Winifred

Books by Doris Miles Disney

Winifred

❊

DORIS MILES DISNEY

PUBLISHED FOR THE CRIME CLUB BY

DOUBLEDAY & COMPANY, INC.

GARDEN CITY, NEW YORK

1976

Library of Congress Cataloging in Publication Data

Disney, Doris Miles.
Winifred.

I. Title.
PZ3.D626Wi [PS3507.I75]   813'.5'2
ISBN 0-385-11545-8

Library of Congress Catalog Card Number 75-25438
Copyright © 1976 by Doris Miles Disney
All Rights Reserved
Printed in the United States of America
First Edition

Winifred

I

"Good night, Mrs. Wheelock," Rita Collins said opening the outside door of the agency, E. Eugene Young, All Lines Of Insurance. "See you in the morning."

The older woman, clearing her desk, looked up and smiled. "Good night, Rita. Enjoy the movie."

"Oh, I'm sure I will." Rita went out to the parking area in front of the small, one-story brick building and got into her car. It was just past five o'clock. The two men at the agency, Young and the salesman, had already left.

The traffic was heavy on Route 1. She had to wait for the light a block away to bring it to a halt before she could turn out onto the four-lane highway and head south. Then she concentrated on driving until she was clear of the sprawling business district of Woodbridge, Virginia, a jungle of brightly colored neon in the early January dusk.

The congestion ended after the last traffic light, giving way to wooded land on either side.

Rita relaxed at the wheel and let her thoughts turn to the evening ahead. She was going with Louise Brooks, her roommate in the house she had inherited from her great-aunt, to see *The Towering Inferno* that night. She had read one of the books the movie was based on and looked forward to seeing it.

After a two-mile drive she moved into the left lane thinking about what to have for dinner as she blinked her direction signal to make her turnoff. There was just enough meat loaf left from last night for the two of them. With a salad and potatoes it would do for a quick meal. What kind of potatoes, though, hashed brown or scalloped? There were packages of both on the shelf.

Rita's street had been no more than a country road ten years ago when she came there to live with her great-aunt Edna, a childless widow, and attend a secretarial school in the area. Thirty years before that, her great-aunt said, when her husband and she built their house, there were only two others along the whole stretch of what was then a dirt road petering out in the woods.

Now there were houses all along it, lights shining from the windows as Rita drove past. At one point a wide slash cut through what was left of the woods, leading to higher ground where a new development of townhouses was being built. The dusk softened its harshness but Mrs. Wheelock had shaken her head over it when she came to dinner last week, deploring the brutality of the bulldozer destroying wild life. "Think of all the poor creatures who lived there," she said. "Their nests and burrows destroyed without warning, very few of them even escaping with their lives."

Rita hadn't thought of it like that; what she had deplored most of all was the coming influx of new people and cars; she was thankful that her house lay well beyond the entrance road to the new development.

Mrs. Wheelock's comments came back to her, however, as she braked for a rabbit that darted out in front of her car and vanished into the ditch on the far side of the road. At least some of the animals had survived.

Rita's house, a Cape Cod, lay around the next curve, with wooded land behind it. Her nearest neighbors in either direction were seventy to eighty feet away, but still she had built a fence across the back and on both sides of the house, taking satisfaction in having her property lines clearly defined.

Lights were on in the living room and upstairs in Louise Brooks's bedroom, her car parked in its accustomed place off the driveway so as not to block Rita's access to the one-car garage. She must have left work early, Rita thought. She usually didn't get home much before six.

Rita pulled up in front of the garage and got out to open the door telling herself, as she often did, that one of these days she would get an estimate on how much it would cost to have a new electronic door installed.

The kitchen was in darkness as she crossed the back yard to the house. She heard water running full force the moment she got inside. She turned on the light. The room was in perfect order just the way she had left it going to work that morning.

She felt a flicker of annoyance. Louise might at least have set the table before she went upstairs to take a shower.

But then, she never did do her share; not in the kitchen or anywhere else in the house. If Rita mentioned her lack of co-operation, Louise's defense was that Rita had her own routine and always wanted things done her way.

What Louise was implying, of course, was that Rita was several years older than she and set in her ways.

But age was a subject that Rita, who would be twenty-nine in June, preferred not to think about.

The shower went off upstairs while she was hanging up her coat in the hall closet.

"I'm home, Louise," she called. "I'll get dinner started. Which would you rather have, hashed brown or scalloped potatoes?"

The bathroom door opened and Louise stuck her head out. "Oh, with the water running I didn't hear you come in. What did you say?"

Rita repeated her question and added, "I'll have dinner ready by the time you're dressed so that we won't have to rush to make the early show."

"Well . . . just a minute till I get my robe on."

Louise spoke on a hesitant note. A moment later, wrapped in a terry cloth robe, she came halfway down the stairs. Fluffing out her damp hair she asked, "Would you mind, Rita, if we went to the movie some other night? It's there all week, isn't it?"

Rita stiffened. "No. It ends tomorrow night."

"Oh. Well, tomorrow night wouldn't work out either because I couldn't skip class for it. We're having a quiz. But maybe we can catch it later at another theater. It's bound to be playing somewhere else soon."

"Why can't we go tonight? You said it would be fine when I suggested it Sunday."

"I know. Thing is, Bill called me at work late this afternoon —so late that I didn't have a chance to call you—and said his boss had two tickets for *Odyssey* tonight at Kennedy Center and something's come up that he can't go so he gave them to Bill who called me right away. Well, what would you have said if you were in my place?" Louise's gaze was fixed apologetically on Rita looking up at her from the foot of the stairs.

"I would have said I already had plans for the evening," Rita made a tight-lipped reply. "After all, an invitation at the last minute—"

"But what other kind could it be when Bill didn't know himself until the last minute that he was going to get the tickets? How could I say no? I didn't want to. You know I adore Yul Brynner and one of the girls at the office said it's a marvelous show. I couldn't bear to miss it."

"I gave up my bowling night because you said this was the only night you could go," Rita pointed out uncompromisingly. "I went to the trouble of finding someone else to take my place and—"

"I'm sorry about that, Rita, but after all, it's just a movie, not like seeing *Odyssey*. Anyway, can't you ask someone else to go with you?"

"This late? No. Besides, the ones I might ask are on my bowling team."

"Well . . ."

The finality in Louise's tone added fuel to Rita's anger. "I think you're being very selfish and inconsiderate," she said. "But then, that's your style, isn't it? It's just like you."

"Rita, I said I'm sorry. We'll see another movie next week if we can't catch this one somewhere. And look, I've got to rush."

Louise turned and started up the stairs. "I left work early so I'd be ready by quarter of six. Bill's picking me up then to allow enough time for dinner before the show."

"That's great. But just make sure you clean up the bathroom before you go. I'm sick and tired of picking up after you. Just because I like things kept neat is no reason for you to act as if I'm the maid around here. After all, it is my house, you know."

Louise, her own temper rising, halted at the top of the stairs. She looked down at Rita's set face and said sharply, "Oh yes, I know whose house it is, no doubt about that. You remind me often enough, God knows. But just let me remind you that I pay my fair share of expenses here—"

"But you don't do your fair share of the housework."

"Yes, I do—or at least I try. It's not my fault that you follow me around doing over what I've already done. There's no law that says I have to measure up to your crazy-clean standards."

"Don't you say that just because I like to keep my things—"

"That's right, *your things,*" Louise shot back. "I could write a book on it but let's forget it for now. Bill will be here soon." She vanished into her bedroom all but slamming the door after her.

Rita gripped the newel post, her rage so violent that after a moment she felt alarmed by the intensity of it. She shouldn't let herself go like this. It was happening to her too often lately.

She dropped her hands to her sides and went back to the kitchen where she sank onto a chair keeping herself, with conscious effort, from gripping the edge of it. Instead, she folded her hands in her lap, not letting them clench into fists, not letting herself spring to her feet and walk the floor.

Gradually, as her rage lessened, resentment took its place. How could Louise, on top of being so selfish about her own plans for the evening, have said such hateful things about the way Rita acted over her house? Why shouldn't she be proud of owning a nice house like this and all the lovely furniture that came with it? Why shouldn't she take good care of it like Aunt Edna before her?

Crazy clean. It wasn't true. Louise was just jealous because it didn't belong to her.

Rita could hear her hurrying back and forth upstairs getting ready for her date with Bill.

She had been seeing him more and more often these past few months since she had come to live with Rita.

What in the world did Bill, attractive, fairly bright, a good government job, see in Louise? If he lived with her as Rita did, picking up after her all the time, putting up with her laziness, the mean little snits she got into like tonight, he would soon drop her. But of course she was on her best behavior with him.

She wasn't even particularly good-looking, a wishy-washy blonde, not even as good-looking as Rita, no beauty herself, was.

But men, for some reason, were drawn to Louise. She never seemed to lack dates if Bill wasn't around.

Rita looked at the clock. Twenty of six. He was due in five minutes. She mustn't give the impression of moping around in the kitchen when he arrived.

She went out the front door at a sedate pace and then ran across the street to get the evening paper out of the tube.

Now when Bill arrived he would find her in the living room, at leisure in her own house, absorbed in the news. A drink would add to the image she wanted to create. She went back to the kitchen before she sat down and made herself a bourbon and soda.

It turned out to be wasted effort. Louise came flying downstairs, coat on, pocketbook in her hand, the moment Bill's car turned in at the driveway. She had the door open before he reached the steps.

"Don't ever complain again that I'm not ready on time," she greeted him gaily. "Right on the dot tonight."

"Good for you," he replied. "Let's go."

He stayed outside. Rita didn't even catch a glimpse of him.

Louise, closing the door behind her, barely glanced into the living room and said on a cool clipped note, " 'Night, Rita."

aware of the growing bond between them. (Or should she be noble and say that Louise had first claim on his affections?)

In the end, whatever attitude she took, Louise would learn to accept the fact that she had lost out to Rita. (A scene along the way, perhaps, with Louise crying and begging her to give Bill up?)

Maybe. But in the end it would make no difference. Louise would resign herself to the first real setback of her life, leaving Rita and Bill to live happily ever after.

Was she too old to have a white wedding? No, not nowadays when people made a point of flouting tradition, doing their own thing.

She could wear her grandmother's wedding veil. There was a picture of her on her wedding day, Marguerita Bruno, bride of John Lathrop, Rita's maternal grandfather.

Her grandmother had been a handsome bride. People who had known her long ago—Rita couldn't remember her herself—said that she resembled her grandmother far more than her mother, who took after the Lathrops, ever had.

Rita had heavier features, though, and her eyes, instead of being dark like her grandmother's, were light gray in unexpected contrast to her olive skin and hair and brows that were almost black.

Steve Morrison, falling in love with her five years ago, had said it was her eyes he had noticed first. "So different," he had said, "when they should be dark to go with the rest of you." And on another occasion, "You look lovely tonight, Rita. Every now and then you're almost beautiful, you know. Other times not even pretty. You're a changeling, that's what you are."

But he hadn't really meant it. He had fallen out of love with her too fast for anything he had said to be true.

He had been like too many other men in her life, giving her a big rush at first and then fading out of the picture. . . .

Not many lately, though. Not any, really, since Pete Randall over a year ago. He, like the others, had since married someone else.

"Good night." Rita did not add, as she normally would, "Have a good time."

She dropped the paper in her lap and listened to the sounds of the car doors shutting, the car backing out onto the street. As it drove off she said aloud, "I hope you have a miserable time, Louise. I hope something happens to spoil the whole evening."

It wouldn't, though. Things always seemed to work out right for Louise.

As they would have, the thought came suddenly, for Dolly if she had lived.

Dolly . . .

Sometimes when her sister came into her mind, Rita couldn't stop herself from going over every detail of Dolly's death. Sometimes it was like the rerun of an old movie inexorably unfolding from the last afternoon of Dolly's life through the long night of the search for her and the terrible irony of what came thereafter.

But tonight she was able to push it out of her mind, turn her thoughts resolutely back to Louise who would probably marry Bill and live happily ever after.

That was the whole story of Louise's life, it seemed. Unlike Rita, she was one of the lucky ones.

The only sound in the quiet of the house was the ticking of the eight-day clock on the fireplace mantel.

Rita glanced at it. Almost six o'clock. She got up and turned on the TV and then let the news pass unnoticed, sipping at her drink, drifting into a fantasy of Louise at last meeting a setback.

Such as, well—such as Bill, interest sparked, having a long talk with Rita one night while waiting for Louise, held up somewhere, to get home.

After that night Bill began to pay more and more attention to Rita until at last he arrived one night when Louise was at class and said he had come to realize that it was Rita, not Louise, whom he loved.

Rita, distressed at first, would finally admit that she, too, was

Rita sighed and looked at the clock again as hunger pangs brought her back from empty memories to the present. Quarter of seven, past time to start dinner.

She got to her feet, folded the unread newspaper neatly, picked up her glass and went into the kitchen to slice the meat loaf, fix the packaged scalloped potatoes, make a salad.

What was Louise eating tonight in some Washington restaurant?

Nothing as uninteresting, certainly, as Rita's meal.

After dinner, after she had stacked the dishes in the dishwasher and made sure the kitchen was in its usual immaculate state, Rita returned to the living room and picked up *TV Guide*.

Might as well see if there was anything she wanted to watch.

II

Mrs. Wheelock and Bob Sutton, the agency's salesman, were already in the office when Rita got there the next morning. Mrs. Wheelock, a widow in her middle fifties, who had been working at the agency for the past twelve years, was always the first to arrive, stopping at the post office on her way to pick up the mail.

She was at her desk opening it when Rita went in, with Sutton lounging in a chair beside her suggesting leads on insurance prospects for her to follow up by phone.

He broke off to say, "Good morning, Rita," and then, as part of their daily ritual, "Hope you got your coffee-making hat on."

"Oh, is there another kind of hat?" Rita asked picking up her cue.

It was her first chore of the morning to make a percolator of coffee, none of them settling for instant.

"Isn't he a nuisance, though, Mrs. Wheelock?" she added, putting her gloves and pocketbook in the bottom drawer of her desk and hanging up her coat. "One of these days I'll tell him to make it himself."

That comment, too, was part of the morning ritual.

There was an electric hot plate, a tabletop refrigerator and a cupboard for cups and plates in a corner off the lavatory.

"How was the movie?" Mrs. Wheelock inquired while the coffee was perking and Rita was setting out cups.

"We didn't go." She gave the older woman an enigmatic

look conveying the message that she would tell her about it later.

"Oh." Mrs. Wheelock turned her attention back to Sutton who was frowning over a letter she had handed him.

"You'd better give this man a call, Bob," she said. "He's not very happy about the way his claim was handled and he's making it his main point that you sold him the policy."

"I'll give him a ring right now," Sutton said getting up from his chair and heading for his cubbyhole office. "Coffee ready yet, Rita?" he asked over his shoulder.

"You can still hear it perking, can't you?" she countered. "I'll bring it in when it's ready."

"Thanks." He vanished through the doorway.

Gene Young arrived. Mrs. Wheelock took the mail that required his personal attention into his private office, larger and more luxurious than Sutton's.

Rita served them all coffee and sat down at her desk with her own cup. Mrs. Wheelock would be in Young's office for the next half hour or more conferring with him on matters connected with the mail. She would end up handling most of the replies herself. She was the mainstay of the agency Rita had learned in her own five years there, could have run it herself and indeed did most of the time. It was so well established by now that Young, about the same age as Mrs. Wheelock, felt free to play golf every day in season and to take two or three week-long vacations in winter to keep up his game, knowing that in Mrs. Wheelock's capable hands the agency ran smoothly without him.

It was a busy morning. When Mrs. Wheelock returned to her desk she was on the phone almost constantly while Young settled down with a second cup of coffee and read the Washington *Post*. Sutton went out at ten o'clock, Rita typed letters and worked on the customers ledger with occasional interruptions to take care of people who came in to pay premiums in cash.

Young left at noon telling Mrs. Wheelock he wouldn't be back that day and at last, after his departure, the office quieted down. Mrs. Wheelock switched the phone over to the answering service and was then ready to lock up and go out to lunch with Rita.

Thrown together as they were for hours every day the older woman had become not just a confidante but a substitute-mother figure to Rita, more open, more understanding than Rita's own mother had ever been.

During lunch she poured out her grievance over last night.

"It was the belittling way Louise did it that hurt the most," she said at the end. "If she'd told Bill she'd call me and ask if I minded and then call him back—it wouldn't have taken five minutes—I would have said yes, of course it was all right as far as I was concerned."

Would she have, though? Mrs. Wheelock wondered. Or rather, would she have said yes graciously or played the martyr?

Rita, for all her good qualities, her readiness to be helpful, always do her share, meet people more than halfway, wouldn't be an easy person to live with. There was that prickly edgy side to her, a—well, was insistence the word for it?—in making sure her own rights weren't infringed upon.

Mrs. Wheelock couldn't help asking herself as she had many times before what had gone wrong in Rita's life. Here she was approaching thirty, basically alone, in constant search of the love she had never, apparently, received from her parents who seemed to be, from Rita's occasional references to them, a very distant reserved pair.

Were they the main reason for Rita's deep insecurity? Mrs. Wheelock herself had seen it crop up in behavior that all too often drove new friends away from her. Particularly men, attracted by her perfectly adequate looks, her outgoing approach to them, and then scared off by the jealous possessiveness that was quick to surface once they showed any real interest in her.

Could these unfortunate personality traits have come just from lack of warmth on her parents' part? They were elderly parents too, meaning to do their best, no doubt, but not able, it seemed, when they lost one daughter, to lavish a double amount of love on the one who was left.

That must be the answer. What else could it be?

Mrs. Wheelock had built up this analysis of Rita little by little over the years as their friendship developed. It had never quite satisfied her but she had to make it do.

Now, weighing her reply, she said, "Yes, Louise should have called you as soon as Bill called her. It would have been more thoughtful on her part. On the other hand—"

"Oh dear." Rita made a face. "On the other hand sounds as if you're taking her side."

"Now really, Rita, aren't you building this up too much?" Mrs. Wheelock's smile softened the reproof. "It's not a question of sides at all. I was just going to say that Louise was probably so excited over the invitation that she didn't think to call you. She wanted to see *Odyssey*, you said—"

"If she had mentioned it to me we could have got tickets for a Saturday matinee."

"But that wouldn't be the same as having Bill take her in the evening, getting dressed up for it and going out to dinner first. She wouldn't want to pass it up just to go to a movie that you could see another time."

Rita thought it over and nodded reluctantly. "Well, it's past and done with, anyway, as far as I'm concerned," she said. "I don't know about Louise, though. She was quite uppity this morning, barely speaking to me."

Rita must have created quite a scene last night for easygoing Louise Brooks to be still harboring resentment over it, Mrs. Wheelock reflected. Rita had probably played down her own part in it in telling the story—people tended to have selective memories over things like that—and was now prepared to feel that it was Louise who was making too much of it.

Mrs. Wheelock changed the subject with mention of her married son in Idaho who had called her last night. They went on to other topics and by the time lunch was over Rita was in good spirits again.

But when she got home that night she found Louise there ahead of her again, packing to leave, a suitcase and tote bag already in the front hall.

While Rita stood taking in the implications of what she saw Louise came downstairs with an armload of clothes over her arm. She laid them over the newel post, looked at Rita coolly and said, "I'm moving out as you can see."

She went back upstairs and came down with another armload of clothes.

"Where are you going?" Rita asked hanging up her coat and advancing into the living room as Louise laid the second armload over the back of the sofa.

"I took some time off today and found an efficiency apartment in Arlington off Glebe Road," Louise replied her tone as cool as her glance. "Bill should be here any minute to help me get moved."

"Oh." Rita spoke with matching coolness. "Just because we had a few words last night?"

"No, not just that." Louise, starting back upstairs halted in the doorway. "That was just the last straw. The whole six months I've been here, Rita, I've been getting more and more fed up with hearing you talk about how this is your house, how everything in it is yours and how I have to be careful of this and watch out for that. I thought, paying my fair share every week, that it was supposed to be my home too. But the way you act, it never has been and never could be. No wonder you can't keep a roommate. No one could live with you, not in this house, anyway."

"What are you talking about?" Rita flared. "You're exaggerating the whole thing, making a mountain out of a molehill. Just because I like the place kept up, looking nice—"

"Have it your way," Louise said with a shrug. "But I'll tell you one more thing you should keep in mind, Rita, if you ever expect to have anyone move in and stay here—don't lean on them too hard; don't be a dead weight hung around their necks."

"What? Me a dead weight? Why I always do more than my share. I always—"

The doorbell rang. Louise turned toward it. "That must be Bill."

Rita rushed out into the kitchen.

The house was small with a simple floor plan; a front hall with a closet beside the staircase, the living room on one side of the hall, dining room on the other; across the back of the house a long kitchen with a doorway into it from either of the two front rooms.

Pressed against the wall by the living room doorway, trembling with outrage, Rita could not help hearing everything that went on, Louise greeting Bill, telling him she had brought all her things downstairs except for her big suitcase and a carton of books. She heard Bill making two trips up and down the stairs, the front door opening and closing as Louise and he went back and forth carrying her belongings out to the two cars.

"That's it, I guess," she heard Louise say at the end and hurried away from the door as Louise came out into the kitchen putting on her coat.

"I'm paid up through Saturday for everything except two toll calls on the next phone bill," she said. "I left a check on the bureau that should cover them. There's nothing else I know of."

"No, there's nothing else."

"Well then, good-by, Rita."

"Good-by."

Louise turned and left. A moment later Bill and she were gone, the front door closing after them, their cars starting up and driving away.

Bill hadn't even come out to the kitchen to say good-by to her.

And just last night she had pictured herself taking him away from Louise.

She had felt drawn to Bill since she met him. Not just for his looks but because the few chances she'd had to talk with him he had listened to things she told him about herself as if really interested, sympathetic even. He had a gentleness about him too. . . .

But he sided with Louise. And now Rita would never see him again.

It happened too often to her. People coming into her life, going out of it for good.

She walked aimlessly around the kitchen and looked at the clock. Close to six. Time to start dinner—except that she didn't feel the least bit hungry. She was too upset over Louise.

No use thinking about it. Read the paper; watch the news instead.

But after that the evening stretched emptily ahead. Call someone, ask them over or go out somewhere?

She didn't feel like it.

In the end, after the news, she heated a can of soup, made a slice of toast and let it serve for dinner.

Funny what a difference there could be in the quality of aloneness, she thought getting ready for bed. With Louise out at night so often Rita was used to being alone at bedtime, preferred it, in fact, since it allowed her leisurely access to the bathroom to have a shower, perhaps, brush her teeth, cream her face, take her time going back and forth to her bedroom.

The difference other nights was that no matter how late Louise stayed out eventually she would be coming home.

But not tonight or any other night hereafter.

Rita was acutely aware of the silence of the house as she brushed her hair in front of her mirror—hair so dark that her aunt Edna would say it had purple highlights in it like the grackles at the bird feeder; and Rita would laugh and point out that at least it didn't have green touches too as they did.

She felt a pang of loss for her great-aunt, her father's aunt, a brisk old lady who had always been kind to her, not only giving her a home while she took her secretarial training but asking her to stay on permanently and get a job in the area.

Rita had welcomed the invitation. They had suited each other and she had no desire to go back to Granville, West Virginia. There she would have had to get a job in the office of the glass company, the town's one industry, or with some bank or small business firm. Even the first year she was at Aunt Edna's her high school friends had begun to scatter. And at home— well, at home in the old-fashioned house on Newton Street—

there were just her father and mother, he retired now, both of them long settled in a humdrum routine that seemed to satisfy them and that she herself had chafed against as far back as she could remember.

Or almost that far beginning not long after Dolly died. Before that home had seemed a brighter, gayer place.

Or had Rita just accepted it as it was in those days? In their early years children tended to accept their home, their parents unquestioningly, not making comparisons, not wishing things were different until they moved into a wider world.

Well, that attitude probably entered into the way Rita had felt at the time but it was only part of it. Home really had been brighter, gayer in Dolly's lifetime because she was bright and gay herself by nature.

Their father had called her his little elf. He could never have called Rita, always tall and big-boned for her age, anything like that. But Dolly was small and slight and quick with unruly light reddish hair, a spatter of freckles, and a mischievous tucked-in smile. Nothing remarkable about her appearance but everyone had noticed Dolly. Everyone had loved her.

Dolly, teetering ahead of Rita that day in an old pair of their mother's high-heeled shoes. . . .

Now don't start thinking about that, Rita admonished herself. Get a book, read in bed for a while.

What was the matter with her, anyway, having to push away thoughts of Dolly two nights in a row?

III

Friday morning Mrs. Wheelock listened to Rita's account of Louise's sudden departure and counseled that she take her time looking for someone else to live with her.

"That is," she added, "if you feel you can get by financially on your own. That nice raise you had before Christmas should help. Or at least give you leeway on asking anyone to come in with you."

"Oh, I can manage all right now by myself. I couldn't have, though, a few years ago. Remember how I started looking for someone to share the house right after Aunt Edna died?"

Louise Brooks had been the fourth roommate since that time, Mrs. Wheelock recalled. The first one had got married but would have left anyway, judging by the fault Rita found with her. The second one, a party-giver, Rita had told to leave. The third one hadn't lasted long either. Now there was the fiasco of Louise's departure.

Rita would probably be better off by herself.

"Take your time," Mrs. Wheelock repeated.

"Oh, I will."

"You're lucky to own a house free and clear of mortgage. You couldn't rent an apartment for what it costs to maintain it."

"I realize that but well—living alone more or less out in the country and with my nearest neighbors all older people with families, it does get lonely at times."

"I know," Mrs. Wheelock said. "I have my own lonely spells too."

It was no answer, they both knew. The older woman had had a husband, a son, a good marriage that lasted nearly twenty years. She had no reason to feel cheated of life, accepting widowhood, making a career for herself at the agency. Just last year she had sold her house and bought a condominium apartment having reached the age, she said, where she wanted to shed some responsibility.

It was midmorning. They had the office to themselves. Rita looked at Mrs. Wheelock, thinking that even in her middle fifties she was an attractive woman with a trim figure, good taste in clothes, a good complexion, and dark blue eyes that contrasted nicely with her soft gray hair.

She must have had chances to marry again in the earlier days of her widowhood, Rita thought. But she was a self-sufficient person, contented with her life, the one real flaw in it the fact that her son and grandchildren were too far away for her to see them as often as she would have liked.

That too, though, she accepted.

"If you're not busy tonight, Rita," she said presently, "how about going to 7 Corners with me after work? I want to look for a coat before they're all picked over in the sales. We could have dinner somewhere and a nightcap afterward at my place before you go home."

"Sounds fine," Rita answered. "I haven't made any plans."

Friday night and no plans. That was too bad, Mrs. Wheelock thought.

They had a pleasant evening together. It was eleven o'clock when Rita got home stopping to pick up the paper and her mail before turning in at her driveway.

She looked at her mail when she went into the house. There were two pieces of it, the light bill—up again this month—and a letter from her mother.

She sat down to read her mother's letter although she didn't expect it to say much. In her parents' uneventful lives there was little news to pass on to her.

This letter, however, ran to two pages.

It began with the statement that both of them were well, up until now not even a head cold. There was still, of course, most of the winter left so they were keeping their fingers crossed. It had snowed last week but the weather this week was quite mild.

Rita skimmed down the page. She could have written the letter herself, so predictable was the content of it.

But the second page was different. It said: "I ran into Mrs. Murray at the drugstore the other day. You remember the Murrays, don't you? They used to live near us until they bought a house the other side of town. Mrs. Murray said their daughter Janet finished her nurse's training in Charleston and is a licensed practical nurse now. She just got a job in an Arlington Hospital and is staying with an elderly cousin until she finds a place of her own. She could have got a job at the hospital here but that didn't suit her. It reminded me of the way you went to Aunt Edna's. Young people are never satisfied to stay home nowadays.

"Mrs. Murray said Janet doesn't know a soul in Arlington and wondered if you would mind getting in touch with her. She's much younger than you, of course, but I said I'd pass on the message. The cousin is Mrs. Thomas Russell, 2901 Charles Square, Arlington. It wouldn't hurt just to call her on the phone. But do what you think best.

Love,
Mother"

Rita laid the letter aside. Janet Murray, years younger. Rita recalled her as a small chubby girl around the corner, perhaps just entering first grade when Rita herself was ready for high school.

They wouldn't have a single thing in common.

Still, if Rita didn't call her, her mother would ask about it in every letter.

Let it go, however, for a couple of weeks. By that time Janet Murray would probably have begun to make friends and found an apartment.

The next day Rita changed her mind. She was up early—she had never been a late sleeper—and had the weekly cleaning finished, the house shining neat by noon, conceding to herself that the work did go faster without Louise underfoot making halfhearted gestures toward doing her share.

But as Rita sat down at the kitchen table with a sandwich and glass of milk for lunch she faced the fact that the rest of the weekend lay ahead and that she had nothing to do except the grocery shopping. An hour at the most would take care of it and then what? She had no plans at all after that.

She thought of Janet Murray. Why not invite her to dinner tomorrow? It wouldn't have to be elaborate. She could make a seafood casserole, a salad, dessert. It would give her something to do and would please her mother who wasn't easy to please.

Besides, she was a little curious herself to see what Janet Murray was like now that she had grown up.

After she had eaten lunch Rita went to the telephone. The directory listed a Thomas Russell at 2901 Charles Square. She dialed the number.

A woman with a quavery voice answered. Mrs. Russell, the elderly cousin, Rita thought.

"Just a minute," she said. "I'll call Janet."

The voice that came on next was as young as tomorrow, an eager lilting voice that said, "Hello, this is Janet Murray."

Rita introduced herself and as she explained how she happened to be calling was certain from the hesitant note in the reply that the girl had no recollection of her or of the Collins family.

"I was only about six or seven, you know, when we moved away," she said matter-of-factly. "The only people I really remember at all were kids my own age. So you see . . ."

"Yes, I see." Rita subdued the edge that came into her voice over the girl's emphasis on how much older she was. Deliberate? No, probably just thoughtless.

She went on to issue her invitation to dinner tomorrow and was mollified at once by the girl's quick acceptance, the warmth with which she said, "Oh, how nice of you. I'd love to come. You'll have to tell me, though, how to get there."

"Do you have a car?"

"Yes. My parents gave me one last summer for my twenty-first birthday."

Another reminder, Rita thought, of the difference in their ages.

"I'd better get a pencil and write down the directions," Janet Murray said. "I'm still such a complete stranger around here that I get lost every time I leave the house." She laughed. "I had to ask twice the other day how to get to the hospital where I start work Monday."

Rita gave her detailed instructions on how to reach her house, adding, "Be sure to check your speedometer when you make the turn off Route 1 south of Woodbridge. After you've gone a little over a mile begin to watch on your left for a brick Cape with a white picket fence around it. You'll see my name, Collins, on the mailbox across from it."

"Oh, I'm sure I'll have no trouble, not with the directions you've given me," the girl said enthusiastically. "What time shall I come?"

"Well, three o'clock, shall we say? I'll plan dinner for around four. You'll want to get home early, won't you, starting on a new job Monday?"

"Why, yes—yes, of course," Janet Murray said but her tone made it plain that it was the last thought in her mind.

"I'll look forward to seeing you. 'By for now."

"Good-by, uh—Rita, you said your name was?"

"Yes." Once again Rita had to keep an edge out of her voice. She wasn't going to like Janet Murray, she reflected as she hung up. Hadn't she been something of a spoiled brat anyway, in her early years?

From the depths of memory Rita dredged up a clearer picture of her, adding to chubbiness big brown eyes, brown hair and a habit of sticking her tongue out at people.

Making out her grocery list, Rita wished she had not invited her to dinner tomorrow.

The best that could be said for it was that it would take up a good part of the day. Winter Sundays tended to drag at times. She always looked forward to spring when she could get outdoors to work in her garden, a labor of love to her.

The phone rang just before she set out on her shopping trip. It was Angie Hunt, a friend she bowled with, asking her to play bridge that evening.

"I hope you don't mind the short notice," she said. "The idea came to me just a little while ago when Stan reminded me he had to go out tonight. I called Dot and Mary Lou and they're free so I thought if you could make it too we'd have a foursome."

"Sounds fine. What time, Angie?"

"About eight o'clock. Gives me time to get Stan off and young Stan in bed."

"Okay. See you then."

Rita hung up. As she turned away from the phone it crossed her mind that if Angie had called her a little earlier she herself, in all likelihood, wouldn't have called Janet Murray. Playing bridge tonight would have been enough to break up the barrenness of the weekend and she probably would have just picked up some books at the library and contented herself with reading and watching TV tomorrow.

The end result might well have been that she never got around to calling Janet Murray at all. Or at least not until she was established to a point where she had no interest in visiting a former neighbor she couldn't even remember.

Well, it was done now. Rita was committed to entertaining the girl no matter how it turned out.

IV

She was a small girl, fine-boned and slim, no trace of childhood chubbiness left, Rita saw, looking out the dining room window when she heard the car arrive shortly before three-thirty the next afternoon.

She still had the big brown eyes but her hair was now ash blond, hanging loose in the current style but not parted in the middle as most of her contemporaries wore it without regard for the flatheaded look it gave them. Hers was drawn straight back, gaining height from the wide green band that kept it off her face and emphasizing the engaging little-girl look she had.

She closed the car door and stood beside it taking a leisurely look around her, assessing, it seemed, the home background of her sometime neighbor.

A very self-confident attitude, Rita thought, crossing the room to the front hall. Most girls in her position, nearly half an hour late in arriving for their first visit, would hurry straight to the door.

Rita didn't like it but opened the door with a welcoming smile when Janet Murray at last rang the bell.

"Come in, Janet," she said. "I hope you didn't have too much trouble finding the place."

"None at all," Janet replied her answering smile displaying a dimple, only one, in her right cheek. "Not with the directions you gave me."

"Good. I was beginning to wonder if I'd missed up somewhere when it got past the time I expected you. Let me have your coat."

"No, it was just that I didn't start out when I should have," Janet said slipping out of her belted camel hair coat.

She might at least add that she was sorry to be late, thought Rita, punctual to the minute herself, as she hung the coat in the hall closet.

Janet, having inspected the outside of the house, engaged in an open examination of the inside, looking over the dining room where Rita had the table set with Aunt Edna's best silver, china and linen and then turning her attention to the living room.

"Sit down and make yourself comfortable," Rita said leading the way into it.

"Thanks." Janet, dressed in a pale green pantsuit that her headband matched, picked out the biggest, deepest chair, Rita's favorite chair, in fact.

"What can I get you to drink?" Rita asked. "I have gin, scotch, bourbon or just plain Coke if you prefer that."

"Oh. You don't happen to have Canadian Club?"

"I'm sorry, no. There's not much demand for it around here."

"A boy I went out with while I was in training always drank it and I got to like it too," Janet said languidly and then, on a resigned note, "Well, I guess I'll have bourbon and soda then."

"Okay." Rita went out into the kitchen. Still a brat, she thought. No manners at all.

She had a pan of hors d'oeuvres ready to put in the oven. She turned on the broiler and set the timer for three minutes before she made the drinks.

While she was busy in the kitchen Janet strolled over to the doorway to continue her inspection of the house. "Very nice," she said her glance taking in the modern equipment and bright color scheme. "How'd you happen to rent a house, though, instead of an apartment?"

"I own it," Rita replied briefly. "It was left to me with all the furnishings a few years ago."

"Oh." Janet raised her eyebrows, impressed in spite of herself. "Lucky you. I've got to start looking for an apartment myself."

"Well, there are lots of them around. You shouldn't have any problem."

The timer buzzed. Rita took the hors d'oeuvres out of the oven and put them on a plate. The drinks were already on a tray. She added the plate to it and said, "Shall we go in and sit down?"

Janet returned to the living room, settling again in Rita's chair, and took her drink and a toast triangle from the tray.

She ate it with great relish and helped herself to more. She seemed to enjoy her drink too regardless of her preference for Canadian Club and was ready for another when Rita suggested a refill.

Meanwhile, she talked steadily about herself, how much she looked forward to living in the Washington area instead of poky old Granville and what a drag it was staying with her elderly cousins.

"Like the grave," she said. "Cousin Catherine putters around all day and Cousin Tom just sits and reads. I can't wait to get away from there."

As Rita was about to serve dinner she asked to use the bathroom and lingered upstairs so long that it became obvious to Rita that she was looking over that part of the house too.

Nosy, she thought, liking her less and less.

When Janet came downstairs and they were seated at the dining room table she said, "How nice to have an extra bedroom. You really are lucky, owning your own house."

Rita's heart sank. She wasn't going to ask if she could move in, was she?

But that wasn't in Janet's mind at all. During dinner she bombarded Rita with questions about various neighborhoods where she might find an apartment within reasonable driving distance of the hospital.

"And fairly central," she said, "so that it will be easy to get to places from it."

"Yes," said Rita watching with envy as Janet accepted a generous second helping of the casserole and another roll. There wasn't an ounce of fat visible on that slim figure whereas she herself, with her big frame, had to count her calories.

But at no time while she ate with appetite did Janet offer a compliment on how good the meal was.

They had coffee in the living room where she reverted to her earlier complaints about the cousins she was staying with.

"You can't imagine how boring it is," she said plaintively, widening her big brown eyes at Rita. "Cousin Catherine expects me to help her every minute I'm there—and not even a dishwasher!—then after they've puttered around all day their idea of a big evening is to stay up to watch the Marcus Welby show."

She threw up her hands to dramatize her despair. "I swear, Rita, I'll be climbing the walls if I don't get out of there before another week goes by."

"It must be a little difficult for them, too, having their routine upset," Rita couldn't resist saying.

"I guess so." Janet's tone dismissed her cousins' reactions to her. "It's all my mother's doing anyway. She insisted on writing to ask if I could stay with them until I had a chance to find a place of my own. Speaking of that, may I ask a favor, Rita?"

"Well . . ." Rita made cautious reply.

"You've lived here so many years, I was thinking after you called yesterday that it would be just great if you'd help me find an apartment. I get overwhelmed myself looking at all the ads in the paper. I expect you could eliminate loads of them at a glance, going by their locations and all that."

"A furnished apartment?"

"Yes, just for a start."

"You think you'll be able to swing it alone? There are roommate referral services, you know, if you want to hold down expenses by sharing with someone."

"I'd rather not. You see," Janet's dimple flashed—it was more intriguing, Rita thought, that there was only one—"I've managed to talk my parents into subsidizing me for a bit until

I can get by on my own. With their help and what I'll be making at the hospital, I can probably go as high as one seventy-five to eighty-five a month."

"Well, you should be able to find something in that range. Nothing elaborate considering what they rent for these days, but something fairly adequate and in a safe neighborhood."

Janet sat forward. "Will you help me look?"

That was how it came about that Rita found herself accompanying Janet on an apartment hunt three nights that week. She met Mr. and Mrs. Russell the first time she picked Janet up at their house. They seemed pleasant and friendly. It was apparent from the many suggestions they offered that they would be as happy to have Janet leave as she would be to get away from them.

Janet was using her, Rita realized, taking her measure from the start. She accepted it resignedly. At least she was in command of the situation, her opinions deferred to.

They went apartment-hunting Monday and Tuesday. Janet turned out to be choosy in spite of her anxiety to have her own place. If she liked the layout of a particular efficiency or one-bedroomer, she didn't like the furnishings. If it wasn't air-conditioned, she wouldn't even look at it. If it was in a high rise, it couldn't be higher than the fourth or fifth floor. Suppose there was a fire, she said; or suppose the elevators didn't work. If the furnishings suited her there weren't enough closets or the outside surroundings weren't right.

Wednesday was Rita's bowling night. When she mentioned being busy that night she hoped that Janet would assume she had a date but Janet came right to the point and asked if she did.

"No, I'm on a bowling team." Janet, Rita thought as she said this, was just about the nosiest person she had ever met.

"Oh." A flat note conveyed Janet's total disinterest. The next moment she asked, "Do you have any special guy, Rita?" and added with a giggle, "Someone who has a friend he could fix me up with, maybe?"

"I'm afraid not."

Driving home after she had dropped Janet off that night, Rita reflected that as far as she was concerned, Janet did not improve on closer acquaintance. Once she found an apartment for her, she would be more than ready to ease out of this sudden intimacy.

In the end it was Mrs. Wheelock, kept informed of the situation, who found an apartment that suited Janet. It was in Falls Church near where she lived herself.

"It's off Route 7," she told Rita Friday morning. "They're garden apartments, air-conditioned, with a swimming pool. The vacancy is on the first floor, a one-bedroomer, nicely furnished, I was told. It's one-ninety a month. Would Janet go that high?"

"I should think so," Rita said. "When can she see it?"

"Any time, I imagine, although it won't be ready for occupancy until Monday or Tuesday, from what the manager said. I met her at a friend's last night. That's how I happened to hear about it."

"It sounds perfect. Do you think we could see it tonight?" Rita laughed. "I can't wait to get Janet settled, get her off my back."

"I'll call the manager right now." Mrs. Wheelock reached for the phone.

At eight o'clock that night Janet signed a year's lease for the apartment and was told she could move in Monday.

She was jubilant when they left. "Exactly what I wanted," she said. "Imagine your friend Mrs. Wheelock, someone I've never even met, finding it after all the looking we did ourselves."

Stopping for a red light Rita said, "Well, would you like to drop by now and see if she's home? It's on our way and it would give you a chance to thank her yourself."

"All right."

Mrs. Wheelock was home and gave them a cordial welcome, interested in meeting Janet who had figured so largely in Rita's conversation all that week.

"I'm pleased it's what you want," she said to her. "And how nice to come and tell me yourself that you've taken it."

Janet didn't enlighten her that it was Rita's suggestion that brought them there. She showed her dimple in a bright smile and replied, "I can't wait to move in."

"Well, come sit down and tell me your plans." Mrs. Wheelock took them into the living room. "Can I get you girls a drink first?"

"If you have Canadian Club—" Janet began but Rita cut in firmly, "Bourbon and soda will be just fine."

Mrs. Wheelock caught the irritated note in her voice and gave her a quizzical look before heading for the kitchen. Janet Murray was really getting on Rita's nerves. It was just as well that the apartment hunt was over.

She had no way of knowing that Rita's irritation had a double edge; not only over the mention of Canadian Club that they had laughed about early in the week but also because Janet had let Mrs. Wheelock think that it was her own idea to stop by and thank her for finding the apartment.

A small omission, a trifle really, Rita acknowledged to herself, but annoying just the same.

When Mrs. Wheelock brought in the drinks Janet took over the conversation, rattling on about her job at the hospital, the people she was meeting there, the supervisor she didn't like, the cute lab technician who had asked her out tomorrow night.

Rita had heard it all before and tried not to listen, studying Janet's animated face and gestures, the dimple that came and went, the little-girl earnestness with which she fastened her big brown eyes on Mrs. Wheelock.

It was too bad, though, that she had to bring complaints about her poor old cousins into her monologue. She could at least pay lip service to their kindness in letting her stay with them or, if not that, make no mention of them at all.

She hadn't a grateful bone in her body, thought Rita. And what an egotist she was.

Mrs. Wheelock, listening politely, shared these thoughts.

Rita would do well to keep the girl at a distance once she was settled in her apartment.

But would she? Just today she had said how relieved she would be to get her off her hands but did she mean it? She needed to be needed.

As soon as they finished their drinks Rita stood up and said, "I'll take you home now, Janet."

"What's the rush?" Janet was enjoying herself with a new audience.

"It's almost nine-thirty and by the time I drop you off and get home myself it will be a lot later. I have a couple of things I want to do before I go to bed."

"Well, all right." Janet got to her feet.

On the way home she said, "Oh, I forgot to tell you my mother called me last night. She's so pleased, Rita, that you've sort of taken me under your wing. She said she called your mother and told her about it and she was pleased too."

Well, that was one plus at least, Rita thought.

"But you didn't tell me," Janet sounded reproachful, "that you were going home next Friday for the weekend. Your mother said that it's your father's birthday a week from tomorrow and that she's having a little party for him."

"I didn't think to mention it."

"Oh." Janet was silent for an interval and then said, "Well, I've been thinking about it and it's given me an idea. As long as you're going anyway, what if I go with you? There are a few things Mama's going to let me have for my apartment and it would save me making the trip by myself."

"All right," Rita said without enthusiasm. But at least it would be company on the long drive.

"What time will you leave Friday?"

"Around three. I plan to take a couple of hours off to get ahead of the commuter rush on 70-S."

"I come off duty at three. Maybe I can get off a little early so that you can pick me up at my apartment. If I can't, I guess you'll have to meet me at the hospital. But we can settle that later. Like Monday night. You'll help me move then, won't you?"

"Yes."

A moment later Janet said pensively, "I never knew until my mother told me last night that you had a sister who died."

"No reason you should have known. You must have been just a baby at the time or not even born."

"Was she older or younger?"

"Two years younger."

"She was killed, Mama said, when—"

"Yes. It was long ago."

Rita's abrupt tone should have silenced Janet but she chose to ignore it. "Her name—Dotty, was it?"

"Dolly," said Rita. And then, pointedly changing the subject, "Do you have much to bring back from your mother's?"

"Just some ornaments and things," Janet replied accepting at last Rita's reluctance to talk about her dead sister.

It didn't matter. Janet could get the whole story from her mother next weekend.

V

When Rita arrived at Janet's apartment at three o'clock the following Friday afternoon there was no sign of her although she had said she was getting off duty early and would be ready on time.

At three-thirty Rita, fuming, contemplated going without her. Before she could make up her mind to do it Janet drove into the parking lot, rushed inside to get her suitcase, put it in back and settled into the seat beside Rita.

For once she was apologetic. "I declare, I don't know why it is that something always seems to hold me up," she said contritely. "It's like Mama always says, 'Janet, you'll be late for your own funeral.' Today, for instance, I was all set to leave and then one of the patients—"

Rita closed her ears to the long involved story poured out by Janet. She drove in stony silence through the heavy late afternoon traffic on the parkway—nourishing her anger with thoughts of how much lighter it would have been forty minutes ago—and spoke in monosyllables when she had to make some sort of reply.

But by the time they had picked up the Beltway and crossed the Potomac into Maryland she let her anger die and began to respond to Janet's overtures.

Yes, she said, they couldn't have asked for a nicer day for the trip; and yes, she had snow tires on her car if they ran into a snowstorm coming back Sunday afternoon.

"We won't, though," Janet stated confidently as they took

the interchange to 70-S. "I'm lucky, you see. I never hit bad weather when I go anywhere." She laughed. "Just remember that and take me with you when you travel in the winter."

God forbid, thought Rita, and said, "Well, it's supposed to be fair and mild, anyway, all weekend."

"That's because I'm with you."

Rita glanced at her. She was only half joking. Apparently, nothing had ever happened to her so far to weaken her belief in her own good luck.

But of course it would, sooner or later. There was satisfaction in dwelling on that prospect.

Janet exclaimed over the heavy fast traffic that kept most of Rita's attention on her driving. "I've never been on 70-S when it was like this before. Well, not many times anyway. It's practically bumper to bumper. Is it regular commuter traffic or because it's Friday?"

"Some of both." Rita found herself adding, "That's why I wanted to get started as early as possible."

Janet made no reply to that. After a moment she said, "Working different shifts at the hospital, I won't often get a whole weekend off like this. When I go home by myself I'll figure it out so that I have time off in the middle of the week or else start early Friday morning."

"That would make it easier," Rita agreed, reflecting that it was another example, however small, of how Janet would always find a way to make things easier for herself.

Past Frederick, Janet began talking about how hungry she was. "I'm practically starved," she said. "I had lunch at eleven and nothing since."

But in spite of her hunger it was long after they left the interstate highway before they found a place in northern Maryland that suited her.

As she gave her order to the waitress Janet said, "Separate checks, please," with the same serene disregard of any return due for a free ride that she had shown a few miles back when Rita had stopped to buy gas.

The latter told herself that she might as well look at the funny side of it, Janet being the way she was.

It was nearly ten o'clock when they got off I-79 in Granville, West Virginia and Rita dropped Janet off at her house where the porch light was turned on and her parents, watching for her arrival, came rushing out to greet her.

After a joyous flurry of hugs and kisses they asked Rita to come in but she refused saying that her own parents would be expecting her.

Downtown Granville was all but deserted, everything closed up for the night, as Rita drove through it to the other side of the town. It had been that way as far back as she could remember. There was no night life in Granville, not much going on at any time, least of all for young people.

Where the business district thinned out she took a right turn toward her parents' house on the outskirts of a residential area and came presently to Newton Street, a dead end with only fields and mountains beyond it. A sinking feeling, all too familiar, assailed her when she reached the white frame house, the last one on the street, and turned in at the driveway.

She pulled over to the side to leave room for her father to go in and out of the garage in back, shut off the motor, and sat for a moment looking at the house.

The porch light was on here, too, but there was no rush to greet her as there had been at Janet's.

She got her suitcase out and squared her shoulders, bracing herself unconsciously not just for the moment of arrival but for the weekend ahead.

Her mother opened the front door as she climbed the steps. "Well, Rita," she greeted her, "I just said to your father that I thought I heard a car drive in."

She was a tall woman, matching Rita's five-eight, with a spare figure and a severely handsome face, relatively unlined under a crown of white hair. She held her cheek forward for Rita's dutiful kiss and stepped back from the doorway.

Rita's father, paunchy and bald, not holding his years as well as his wife, came from the living room to greet her.

They shook hands; she gave him a dutiful peck too.

"Have a good trip?" he inquired. "We thought you'd get here a little earlier."

"Friday night traffic," she reminded him.

"Ah yes. Here, I'll take your bag upstairs." He went ahead of her with it and set it down in her room turning on the light.

"There you are," he said. "Come down when you're ready."

As his step receded on the stairs Rita carried her suitcase over to a chair and opened it. She had brought little—just the essentials and a frilled blouse to put on with the suit she was wearing for her father's birthday dinner tomorrow night.

She took her time unpacking, though, hanging up her blouse and robe in the closet—most of the space pre-empted long ago by her mother for off-season clothes—and then, after using the bathroom, was ready to go downstairs.

She lingered in the doorway first looking around the room that had been hers from infancy onward, a medium-size room furnished with simple pine pieces, a slipper chair added in later years, childhood toys and books put away in the attic.

It had a stark unused look, she thought; it was almost like Dolly's room across the hall.

She couldn't imagine ever occupying it again except for an occasional visit such as this.

She turned out the light and went downstairs.

Her parents were in the living room, as little changed as Rita's bedroom. It had the same varnished oak woodwork and floor that went back to when the house was built over sixty years ago; the same patterned rug, faded now, that had been new when Rita was a child; the same slipcovered sofa and chairs—but the list was endless, including the flowered vase on the fireplace mantel; and over it the oil painting of Dolly.

There was one of Rita too, over the sideboard in the dining room. Both had been painted the last summer of Dolly's life by an itinerant artist spending a summer in the West Virginia mountains earning his way from town to town with brush and easel.

Not a good artist—Rita had never liked the painting he had

done of her—but somehow he had captured the essence of
Dolly, the bright, gay look she had, the faint tucked-in smile of
a Hummel figurine.

Rita turned her gaze away from it and sat down on the sofa
facing the two front windows. Between them hung another oil
painting of a ship in full sail with a flock of sea gulls hovering
around it. Rita had counted the sea gulls in her childhood;
there were seven of them then and seven now as she automat-
ically made the count.

Her parents each had their own chair, her father's with an ot-
toman on which his slippered feet rested, her mother's a wing
chair so placed that when she raised her eyes she was looking at
Dolly's picture.

"Can I fix you something to eat, dear?" her mother asked.
"There's ham left from dinner—"

"No, thank you," said Rita. "We stopped for dinner on the
way."

"Oh yes, you had Janet Murray with you. Her mother called
to tell me you were giving her a ride home. I haven't seen Janet
for two or three years but last time I saw her I thought she'd
grown up to be a real pretty girl."

"Yes, she certainly is."

"Is she settled in her apartment now?"

"Yes. I helped her move in."

Janet's apartment served as a topic of conversation for the
next few minutes. Then Rita asked, "How's everything with
you people?"

"Same as always," her father replied. "We rub along."

His pipe and tobacco lay on the table next to his chair along
with the copy of *Field & Stream* that he had been reading
when Rita arrived. Fishing and hunting had always been his
chief hobbies. Nowadays, retired from the glass company where
he had worked his whole adult life, he had taken up chess,
playing once or twice a week with his brother-in-law, also retired. Rita's mother belonged to a bridge club and was active in
the women's guild at her church.

Such was the pattern of their lives, suited to their needs.

There was no place for Rita in it nor did she have any desire to seek one.

They were quiet people. Their house was the same. It had been that way all of Rita's growing-up years. She hadn't often invited school friends there, not because her parents made them feel unwelcome but because Rita herself was reluctant to have them. There was never any laughter in the house, any bustle of activity or sense of things happening.

It hadn't always been like that, she reflected, her thoughts turning once again to those earlier days when there had been some liveliness, some fun, with plans to do this or that, go on a picnic, take a trip to Charleston, visit a cousin in Morgantown.

But all that was before Dolly died.

She shall have music—or was it make music?—wherever she goes. That was Dolly straight out of a nursery rhyme. She shall make brightness wherever she goes. . . .

But then she had gone forever and this house almost overnight had changed. Her parents had withdrawn into their deadly quietness, built a wall around themselves that shut out the rest of the world, including Rita.

How long had it taken her after the great change came and she herself was trying to cope with it, bogged down in pain and guilt and bewilderment, to realize that her parents could not forgive her for being alive while Dolly was dead?

Not too long, probably. Children sensed things. In some part of herself she had always known that Dolly was her parents' favorite. If taxed with it, they would have been firm in denial. You are both our daughters; we love you both the same they would have said—and possibly believed—before Dolly's death.

But how could that ever be true of any parents? Aside from the special relation between them, their children and they were also individual human beings reacting one to another.

In her case, her parents had loved Dolly more than they loved her.

Had her awareness of that played any part in what had happened to Dolly?

How many times had she asked herself that sorry question over the years? She would never be able to answer it.

While these thoughts went in and out of her head Rita made conversation, asking about her aunt and uncle and various neighbors, making small talk about her job and her own activities.

The light beside her father's chair showed up the freckles on his bald head. The fringe of reddish hair around it seemed even grayer than the last time she had noticed it. He would be sixty-nine tomorrow. Her mother was five years younger. They were married ten years when she was born and two years later, Dolly. Two daughters born in close succession after all their years of a childless marriage must have had a cataclysmic effect on whatever kind of a life they had established together.

Her father had called her his little bambino, teasing her about her dark coloring inherited from her maternal grandmother.

He had called Dolly his little sunbeam.

Dolly had been a changeling in this house whereas Rita herself had been a solemn quiet child, true daughter of her parents.

There was irony in that.

At eleven o'clock, suppressing a yawn, her mother said, "Hadn't you better be getting to bed, dear? You must be tired after your long drive."

Rita, running out of small talk, was thankful to agree.

Saturday was a clear sunny day, not too cold. She escaped from the house for an hour by taking a walk. She might have turned toward town but instead turned the other way toward the mountains, the railroad trestle, although she did not go near it.

Her aunt Mary and uncle Roger, her father's sister and brother-in-law, and a widowed cousin came to the birthday dinner that night. There was cake and ice cream and even a bottle of white wine, a rare festive touch, to accompany the crown roast of lamb.

Rita presented her father with the shirt she had brought

him. After dinner he played chess with his brother-in-law while the four women played bridge.

At eleven-thirty the party broke up and the high spot of the weekend was over.

Rita called Janet at noon the next day to remind her that they were to leave at two o'clock. "Please try to be ready," she said. "I don't want to be late getting home."

"I'll be standing at the door," Janet replied. "Just wait and see."

She wouldn't be, of course. But almost ready, perhaps. It was funny, Rita thought when they finished talking, how well she felt she knew Janet on relatively short acquaintance. But then it didn't take long to figure her out.

Rita was ready to leave after one o'clock dinner, packed in five minutes to be on her way.

"I don't suppose we'll see you again until Easter, will we?" her mother asked proffering her cheek for a good-by kiss.

"Not unless you visit me some weekend in between."

"Well, you know how it is. Charleston's about as far as I can get your father to drive these days."

The reply was as meaningless as Rita's invitation—if it could be called that. They hadn't been to Woodbridge since Aunt Edna's funeral.

"We'll make it sooner or later," Rita's father said.

But they never would, she knew. They didn't miss her that much.

She picked up her suitcase and when her father would have taken it from her said, "Oh, don't bother, Dad. It's light as a feather, hardly anything in it."

"Well, all right." He gave her a peck on the forehead. "Drive carefully now."

"I will."

They stood in the doorway as she started her car and backed out onto the street. A last wave from them then and the door closed.

By contrast, Janet's whole family and a good-looking young

man came spilling out of the house when Rita stopped in front of it, all except Janet herself.

Each one carried something; the young man, introduced as Don somebody, placed Janet's stereo carefully on the back seat, her mother carried a table lamp, her father and preteen brother cartons of record albums.

More trips back and forth were made with an electric toaster, linens and miscellaneous equipment. The back seat and trunk were packed full before Janet came out of the house at her leisure, the young man carrying her suitcase and somehow wedging it into the trunk.

Rita foresaw herself having to help unload it all when they got to the apartment.

Everyone seemed to be talking at once, particularly the parents paying homage to Janet, obviously a doted-upon daughter —spoiled-rotten daughter would be more like it, Rita thought tartly—with Janet taking their homage as no more than her due.

When she was finally seated beside Rita she rolled down the window on her side for last giggly scraps of conversation with the young man who held her hand while he kissed her good-by and said he would call her during the week.

He went back to join her family as Rita started the car. They all stood at the curb waving and calling good-by, the mother throwing kisses until Rita's car was out of sight.

"Isn't Don the cutest thing you ever saw?" Janet said. "I sent him a card that I was coming and heavens, he had every minute of the weekend lined up with things for us to do. We had a ball!"

She bubbled on about the party they'd gone to Saturday night in Morgantown where Don attended the university, the school friends she had seen, the brunch one of them had given for her yesterday.

They were back in Maryland, West Virginia well behind them, before she got around to asking, "How did your weekend go?"

"It was pleasant," Rita answered.

Their one stop on the way home was to buy gas. When they reached Janet's apartment Rita, just as she had foreseen, had to help her carry in the accumulation she had brought from home.

When it was done Janet thanked her and said good night, not asking her to sit down and stay awhile.

Not that Rita wanted to. The apartment, messy enough when they went into it, dirty dishes in the kitchen, the bed unmade, odds and ends scattered around, was twice as bad with all the packages and cartons added to it.

But Janet should at least have offered a drink, Rita thought going back to her car. Or a cup of coffee. Something. She hadn't wanted to make the effort, not knowing it would be refused.

Easter trip home, Rita told herself, she would make sure she went alone.

VI

Monday morning she gave Mrs. Wheelock a caustic account of Janet's shortcomings as a traveling companion beginning with her lateness when they left Friday.

Mrs. Wheelock could hardly believe the story. "She didn't offer to pay for any of the gas or buy your dinner?"

Rita laughed with some chagrin. "She never opened her pocketbook except to pay for her own meal."

"What a taker that girl is," said Mrs. Wheelock. "The best thing you can do is stay away from her."

"I know. I intend to from now on."

Rita, as it turned out, wouldn't have given much thought to Janet anyway for the next few weeks, not with Ted Parker coming into her life the very next day.

She was alone in the office that Tuesday morning when a salesman from the Chevrolet agency called. He had just sold a car, he said, to a Mr. Theodore Parker, a civil engineer from Wilmington, North Carolina, who had come to the area recently to supervise the construction of a new shopping complex off 95. He carried his insurance with The Hanover Insurance Company and would like his coverage transferred to his new car when he took possession of it tomorrow. The salesman had recommended the Young agency as representing Hanover in Woodbridge.

Rita took down all the information the salesman rattled off but when he asked if the whole thing could be taken care of over the phone, she said, "Well, yes, except that Mr. Young always asks that the policyholder stop by here and sign a written request for a transfer. It's usually sent on to the home office."

That was how, half an hour later, Ted Parker came into her life.

He was somewhere around thirty, tall—Rita, conscious of her own height always noticed that first in a man—brown hair and eyes, dressed in modishly conservative clothes. After his height, she noticed his receding hairline next. For the rest, he had an unremarkable face. Then his warm smile introducing himself, transformed his whole appearance. He really was quite good-looking, she decided.

He repeated her name when she gave it and asked him to sit down by her desk. "Rita Collins," he said. "Easy to remember." He glanced at her ringless left hand as he seated himself and added, "Miss Collins or do you prefer Ms.?"

"Miss is just fine." She smiled. "In any case, I don't think Mr. Young would go for Ms."

"Male chauvinist pig?"

"Yes indeed. He turns purple over some of the sillier aspects of Women's Lib."

"Oh. I only turn pink myself. For instance, 'Chairperson' does it to me."

They both laughed. He might have been out of there in five minutes, his business concluded, but he was still sitting by Rita's desk fifteen minutes later when Mrs. Wheelock returned from seeing a policyholder.

Rita's animation as she introduced Ted Parker did not escape the older woman's attention. Too much animation, she thought; and then, Oh, dear.

Thursday morning he called Rita at work. "I hope you don't mind," he said. "I would have called you at home but there are so many Collinses in the phone book I couldn't figure out, not knowing your address, which one you were."

"Well, you wouldn't have found me anyway. It's a different phone company here and we have our own directory. I'm listed as R. Collins, Dorset Road."

"Well, no wonder I couldn't locate you. What I wanted to

ask was if, by any chance, you're free for dinner tonight. If you are, I thought it would be nice to go somewhere in Washington to start breaking in my new car."

"Oh, I'd love to."

Mrs. Wheelock looked up from her desk catching the eager note in Rita's voice.

"Good. Seven o'clock, say? You'd better give me complete instructions, though, for getting to your place. I still get lost quite easily around here."

Janet, Rita remembered, had said much the same thing when she invited her to dinner.

When he had written down what she told him he said, "So you live in a real honest-to-God house. I assumed you had an apartment." He paused and then asked tentatively, "Do you live with your parents?"

"Oh no, they're in West Virginia. It's my house. It was left to me. I live by myself."

"Well, what d'you know. A girl who owns her own house."

Rita laughed. "You won't be so impressed when you see it. It's a small house, only five rooms."

"I'll look forward to seeing it just the same. And you."

"Seven o'clock then." Rita spun around in her swivel chair after she hung up and exulted to Mrs. Wheelock, "That was Ted Parker who was here the other day. He's asked me out to dinner tonight. Isn't that great?"

"Yes, except that, well—" the older woman hesitated, "you don't really know anything about him, do you? Coming from North Carolina, he might have a wife there who'll be joining him later. He's certainly old enough to be married and have children too."

But Rita's pleasure could not be dampened by any words of caution. "Oh, I'm sure he's not," she said. "He seems so nice. Not at all the type to be cheating on a wife." Excitement had brought color to her cheeks. "What shall I wear, Mrs. Wheelock? How about the winter white I bought for the Youngs' Christmas party? It's not too dressy, is it?"

"No indeed. Just right, I should think."

Rita ran her hands through her hair. "It looks a sight," she said. "Is it all right for me to take an hour off sometime today if my hairdresser can fit me in?"

"Yes, of course." Mrs. Wheelock sighed in resignation as Rita reached for her phone. It was no use wishing she hadn't made herself instantly available for dinner with Ted Parker. That was one of her problems with men, never playing the least bit hard to get. And now that she had reached the panic stage over not being married it was worse than ever.

But if only she wouldn't let it show so much, scaring them off.

No matter how tactfully this was pointed out to her it didn't do a bit of good.

It was funny, Mrs. Wheelock reflected while Rita was making her hair appointment, how some girls seemed to lose out with men while others could pick and choose.

In her own young days she had been fortunate enough never to lack beaus. Looking back, she wasn't sure why. She certainly hadn't been outstanding in looks or in personality. But then, most women weren't.

How many million words had been written analyzing the mating process? Psychiatrists, psychologists, counselors of every sort had had their say but none had come up with a clear-cut answer to what brought people together.

Rita hung up at that point in Mrs. Wheelock's musings and said triumphantly, "They'll squeeze me in at four-fifteen. If I'm home by six that will give me an hour to get ready before Ted arrives."

Ted. Was she thinking of him as Ted already with no awareness of how possessive it sounded?

Mrs. Wheelock sighed again in resignation and said, "I hope you'll have a wonderful time."

"Thank you." Rita turned happily back to her desk.

She spent a very pleasant evening with Ted Parker, beginning with the drive into Washington in his new car to a Capitol Hill restaurant she had suggested when he reminded her that she knew more about the city than he did.

As they sat facing each other at a table, Rita encouraging him to talk about himself, she found him almost handsome. His receding hairline, for example, began with a clearly defined widow's peak and he didn't let it grow too long in back to compensate for the loss in front. He had beautiful teeth, close-set ears. Just as she noticed height, she also noticed ears because her own stood out too much and she had to make sure her hair covered them.

On his part, Ted Parker found her better-looking than he had thought the other day, her eyes bright, the white dress she wore setting off her dark hair and olive complexion.

He would have laughed if he had known how closely their thoughts paralleled each other. Rita wouldn't have, taking herself too seriously for that in her association with men, a trait Mrs. Wheelock had overlooked when assessing her earlier in the day.

Ted Parker talked readily enough about himself, his family, his education, his job, expanding under her interest.

What pleased Rita most was that he would be back and forth between his company's home office in Wilmington and Northern Virginia for at least a year and possibly as long as eighteen months.

He had had assignments of that sort before, he told her; and as his experience grew, there would probably be more of them when the Arlington complex was finished.

He seemed to have a promising future with his company, she thought.

Would she mind moving around like that herself from one job to another? No, not really. It might be interesting, new places, new people.

Mrs. Theodore Parker . . .

"We're practically gypsies, my husband and I. He's a civil engineer, you see, and his company sends him all over the country. . . ."

She brought her thoughts back to an anecdote he was relating about his brother.

The openness with which he talked removed the small nagging doubt Mrs. Wheelock had instilled on his marital status. There were no blank spaces in what he told her that left room for a wife in the background.

Particularly reassuring toward the end of dinner was his wry reference to having been engaged two years earlier. "There are a lot of afterthoughts when you get that far toward marriage and it doesn't work out," he said and then, "What about you, Rita? Have you been through anything like that?"

She could hardly say she had never had a serious proposal of marriage. Instead, she said enigmatically, "Well, not exactly. It didn't get as far as a formal engagement. I had second thoughts, too, you see." She firmed the statement into an outright lie. "Twice with two different men."

"Twice?" He raised his eyebrows but after a moment nodded understandingly. "It is a big step, isn't it? And sometimes, the longer you wait the harder it is to take."

That wasn't encouraging to any view of Ted Parker as a matrimonial prospect. But their waiter came just then to clear away their plates and Rita dismissed it from her mind.

Conversation continued to flow easily after that interruption but in different channels. They sat so long over dessert and coffee that it was nearly eleven o'clock by the time they got back to Rita's house.

She invited him in for a nightcap. When he left, not wanting to see him go without a commitment for the future, she said on impulse, "If you're not busy Sunday, Ted, would you like to come have supper with me? Nothing elaborate—we might even have it here in the living room in front of the fire and perhaps play Scrabble afterward."

He had mentioned during dinner that he liked Scrabble.

"Thanks, that's fine with me," he said. "What time?"

"Around five-thirty, maybe?"

"Okay, see you then."

She walked to the door with him. He kissed her lightly. "It's been the nicest evening I've had the whole month I've been here," he said.

She went to bed with her head full of dreams.

Tomorrow she would buy a Scrabble set.

VII

There was no opportunity Friday morning to tell Mrs. Wheelock about her date with Ted Parker. The older woman was in Young's office until almost noon and Rita herself was busy typing up new policies, taking incoming calls and bringing accounts up to date.

But at lunch there was time to go into every aspect of what a perfect evening it had been.

The way she talked, the bright look on her face took years off her appearance, made her seem as artless as a girl just out of her teens, Mrs. Wheelock thought.

But she wasn't. She was a woman approaching thirty and at that age artlessness became pathetic.

If only it would work out for her this time, though . . .

Rita brought into her recital all that Ted Parker had told her about his background stressing the fact that he wasn't married.

"Did he tell you how old he is?" Mrs. Wheelock asked.

"No, not right out, but putting things together, when he was in college, how many years he's been working and so on, he's probably around thirty-one or thirty-two." Rita smiled. "Just the right age for me, wouldn't you say?"

"Yes, except that you have to keep it in mind that when a man past thirty is still a bachelor, he's no easy catch."

"I know. But nothing ventured, nothing gained."

"Did he mention seeing you again?"

"He's coming to my house this Sunday. I invited him to supper."

Mrs. Wheelock kept her thoughts on that to herself.

The Sunday night supper, however, turned out to be a great success, Rita reported happily the next day. She had served country ham and salad, apple cake with ice cream. Ted had had two helpings of everything. They had played Scrabble afterward. And Thursday night he was taking her to a movie.

"He plays bridge," she continued. "I told him that Angie Hunt and her husband were real addicts and that I'd fix it up with them for the four of us to play some night soon."

Once again Mrs. Wheelock kept her thoughts to herself. There was no point in voicing them. Rita wouldn't—or was it couldn't?—be made to understand that men didn't like having their lives taken over, their courting done for them.

But during the next two weeks or so Mrs. Wheelock began to wonder if Ted Parker wasn't an exception to the rule. He seemed to go along unresistingly with Rita's plans, playing bridge with her friends, taking her to the movies and the Hayloft Dinner Theater, accepting two invitations to dinner at her house.

Rita came to work one Friday morning and said that the two of them were going to the Chinese Exhibit at the National Art Gallery Saturday afternoon.

"I told Ted how much you and I enjoyed it when we went just after Christmas," she said. "And that if he didn't get to see it pretty soon he never would. So we're going tomorrow. I look forward to seeing it again myself."

What a glowing look she had, Mrs. Wheelock thought, when she talked about Ted Parker.

Rita's phone rang. It was Janet Murray to whom she had scarcely given a thought since their trip to West Virginia.

"Hi Rita," she said. "This is Janet. How've you been?"

"Fine. And you?"

"Oh, I'm fine too. Been meaning to call you but you know how it is. I've been so busy—"

"So have I," Rita put in crisply. Did Janet think she had been sitting by the phone waiting to hear from her?

"We must get together soon, plan something," Janet went

on. "Meanwhile, though, I was wondering if you could help me out."

So she wanted something. Of course. Otherwise she wouldn't have called.

"I'm having some people from the hospital over tomorrow night for a potluck supper—"

It would be potluck, Rita thought acidly.

"—and I need a big coffee pot. My new boy friend—we're not up-to-date on each other, are we?—loathes instant and I promised him real coffee. He's an intern at the hospital, you see, and says he has a cup of instant thrust at him every time he turns around. My percolator only holds six cups and I thought that maybe, with all the things you got from your aunt, you might have something bigger."

Rita almost said no. But she did have a big old-fashioned electric coffee pot and it went against her nature to be unobliging. So she replied, "Well, yes, I have one that makes twenty-four cups. Will that do?"

"That would be just fine. There'll only be ten of us altogether." Janet paused. "I don't suppose that by any chance you'll be over this way to drop it off, will you?"

The brass of it! "No," Rita said firmly. "If you want it you'll have to come and get it."

"Oh. How about tomorrow afternoon then?"

"I have a date then. You'll have to pick it up tonight or tomorrow morning."

"Well, better be tonight," Janet said on a resigned note. "Around eight. 'By for now."

Rita said good-by and relayed the conversation to Mrs. Wheelock.

Even as they both laughed over it Mrs. Wheelock said, "I was hoping you'd seen the last of her."

"So was I," said Rita.

She had the coffee pot out on the hall table at eight o'clock that night. It was nine when Janet appeared and sat down in the living room prepared to stay for a while.

She was full of her own affairs, dates she'd had lately, how much she liked her new boy friend, Sam Richards, the intern at the hospital. Finally she asked, "What are you doing for excitement these days, Rita?"

"Oh, I've been going out quite a bit myself. As a matter of fact, I have a new beau too."

"Really? What's his name and what is he like?"

It became Rita's turn to talk, telling Janet how attractive Ted Parker was, what a responsible job he had, what good prospects for the future, how often she was seeing him.

Janet, a little impressed, eyed Rita speculatively. "You know, somehow I thought you—well, didn't do much dating."

"Did you? I go out a good bit. I'm choosy, though. Past the stage where I'll go out with just anybody the way younger girls —your age, Janet—will."

"Heaven's sake, I don't have to grab at—"

But Rita, warming to her own defense, overrode her. "I haven't had any real shortage of men in my life," she said. "As a matter of fact," her firm tone lent weight to the lie, "I'd just broken off with someone when I met you last month. Because I'm so choosy. Right now Ted seems right for me. But who knows, next month or the month after—" she shrugged. "Sooner or later, of course, I'll have to settle down. It doesn't hurt, though, to take your time."

"But if you take too much time you might get left," Janet retorted, piqued by Rita's patronizing tone.

"Oh, I'm not worried about that," Rita stated languidly. The tale she had told Ted Parker popped into her mind. "I've come close to marriage twice already and backed off."

"Really?" Janet looked even more impressed. She was seeing her through new eyes, Rita reflected with satisfaction. Not as on the edge of being passé but as someone so sure of herself with men that she could take all the time there was to settle on a husband.

She felt so superior at the moment that as Janet stood up to leave she heard herself say, "Why don't we get together here for a foursome soon? Ted and I and you and whoever you'd like to bring. Have pizzas or something like that."

"That would be great," said Janet preceding her into the hall. "Why don't we set the date now? I'll bring Sam Richards."

But Rita was already in retreat from her impulsive invitation. "Well, I'll have to check with Ted first, find out when he's free. And you'll have to check with Sam, won't you?"

"Oh, whatever I say will be fine with him." She picked up the coffee pot and added, "I'll mention it to him tomorrow night and you can check with your guy."

"Yes," said Rita on a falling note.

Now why had she got into that? she asked herself standing in the doorway until Janet started her car.

She knew why, though; showing off to Janet, trying to hold her own with her.

Well, she needn't follow through on the invitation. She would just stall Janet off until the whole thing was forgotten.

But she was underestimating the younger girl's persistence, her curiosity about Rita's new beau. Janet called her the following Tuesday, chatted about what fun her potluck supper had been and then said, "Oh, I told Sam how you'd suggested we all get together for a foursome at your house, and how nice it is with a fireplace and all. He's looking forward to it. He said he never gets invited to anyone's house around here, just apartments. I told him maybe you'd have a fire unless it's too warm a night."

"Well, I didn't think to mention it to Ted yet," Rita said. "I will, though, this weekend."

"Oh, you won't see him until then?" The implication was clear; since this was only Tuesday, Ted Parker wasn't exactly at Rita's beck and call.

"Tomorrow night's my bowling night and Ted will be out of town Thursday. But he's taking me out to dinner Friday night and I'll bring it up then."

"Fine. Just let me know. I'll bring back your coffee pot when we come."

"It doesn't matter. I rarely use it."

"You'll call me as soon as you've talked to Ted?"

"Yes." What a nuisance Janet was, Rita thought as she hung up. She had the hide of an elephant pushing like that.

Rita's attitude toward Janet was reflected in her tone when she told Ted Parker about the prospective foursome at dinner that Friday night.

"I can't get out of it now," she said. "But hasn't she got a nerve?"

He laughed. "Well, just get it over with. Make it Saturday night, a week from tomorrow. I may be away most of the week but I'll be back by then."

"All right," Rita said resignedly.

Afterward she would agonize over how readily she had arranged the foursome with no thought of Janet as competition— how could she have been so stupid?—with no feeling stronger than exasperation at herself over what she had got into, showing off to Janet.

If only she had put Janet in her place, said flat out that she was too busy to plan a get-together right now, that she would call her later on . . .

Rita would lie awake nights making up statements to Janet that would have kept her from ever laying eyes on Ted Parker.

Instead, Janet arrived the following Saturday night with her date, a large amiable young man whom she introduced with a giggle saying, "You don't have to call him Dr. Richards, though. He answers to Sam."

"Come on now, Janet," he protested, shaking hands with Rita and Ted Parker, adding, "She's the one who makes a big deal over the doctor bit. Getting back at me, I reckon, because I give her orders at the hospital."

Janet made a face at him and then exclaimed to Rita, "Oh, I forgot to bring back your coffee pot. Imagine!"

"It doesn't matter," Rita replied, her heart already beginning to sink over her folly in bringing Janet and Ted together.

Janet had never looked prettier, her dimple in full play, big shining eyes fixed on Ted Parker as she said, "It's so nice to meet you after all Rita's told me about you, how you're an engineer in charge of building a big shopping plaza in Arlington and all that. But," she fluttered her lashes at him, "I thought you'd be a lot older with an important job like that."

Rita's face went hot with embarrassment. How could Ted smile at the brat and look flattered? Didn't he see the malice in it, the intent to show up Rita for bragging about him?

If he did, he gave no sign of it, helping Janet off with her coat, asking her what she would have to drink when she was seated in the living room.

She was wearing a dress tonight instead of a pantsuit; a blue dress, fluffy, feminine, displaying her pretty legs.

She went through her routine about liking Canadian Club. "But Rita never seems to have it"—a plaintive note—"so I'll have bourbon and soda, please."

That was what Sam Richards would have too. But he didn't count, settled in a chair filled to capacity, commenting cheerfully on how good it was to have a fire.

Ted Parker had offered before their arrival to go out for the pizzas Rita had ordered. When it was time to pick them up Janet said she would keep him company as long as Rita would be too busy getting everything else organized. "You help her, Sam, hear?" she said while Ted Parker held her coat for her. "We'll be right back."

They could have been back in fifteen minutes but were gone more than twice that long.

It seemed forever to Rita.

"We had to wait and wait," Janet said on their return.

Rita reacted by asserting her rights with Ted Parker, assigning him the role of host, turning desperately gay, almost strident in her efforts to hold his attention.

Janet never stirred from the chair where she curled up distributing her smiles and attention on both men and taking as little notice as possible of Rita.

Who had lost out to her, she knew with heartsick certainty, long before the evening at last came to an end.

VIII

But Ted Parker did not drop Rita without first making a gesture of sorts. He called a few days later to say he was going home for the coming weekend and would call her when he got back. He would not, however, let her pin him down to any definite commitment.

Still, hope stirred in Rita, easing a little the dead weight of loss she carried around inside her. Maybe, she told herself, she was wrong about the finality of Saturday night; maybe, when it was over, and Ted had a chance to think about what a blatant play Janet had made for him, it had turned him off; maybe he had been especially attentive to her only because she was Rita's guest. He couldn't, after all, have said no when she offered to go get the pizzas with him.

But Rita had to discard this last possibility as too optimistic, too far removed from the bitter realities of Saturday night.

It was better to settle for her first hypothesis: that when he had thought over what a shallow obvious type Janet was, he had realized his response to her was just a temporary aberration; that Rita, on a solider basis, had a great deal more to offer him.

Ted Parker, with well-meant politeness that only prolonged for Rita the misery of alternating hope and despair, called her after his weekend trip home and suggested dinner Thursday night.

Rita bought a new dress and had her hair done for the occasion. They went, on what he knew was to be their last date, to the same Washington restaurant they had gone to on their first one.

She tried to act as if nothing had changed and was so transparent in her eagerness to please that he felt embarrassed for her.

Janet was not mentioned but her invisible presence hovered over them.

There would have been no comfort for Rita if she had known that Ted Parker had taken Janet's measure the night he met her; that while her looks and fresh young insouciance attracted him he had no more intention of becoming seriously involved with Janet than he had had with Rita.

He had found Rita as obvious, in an entirely different way, as Janet. His newness to the area had played a part in his first asking her to go out with him and continuing to see her. He had enjoyed her company well enough but by the time he met Janet he had begun to get annoyed over the way she took charge, making plans for them, trying to arrange their next date every time he saw her.

It was plain that she wanted to get married whereas he didn't. He was thankful now that he hadn't made any serious attempt to go to bed with her; at least she had no claim of that sort on him.

With Janet Murray, on the other hand, he could see no immediate problems. He didn't know yet what she had in mind for him—most girls had thoughts of marriage, whether they admitted it or not, didn't they?—but Janet was still too young, with too much going for her, to feel any need to rush things. At least he hoped so.

He was taking her out again tomorrow night.

He had Rita home before ten o'clock that night saying no, he wouldn't come in for a nightcap; saying no, she'd better not fix up a bridge date with the Hunts next week because he would probably be out of town.

He kissed her good night perfunctorily at the door and said, "Had a nice evening, Rita. I'll be in touch."

She went to bed in tears. But still, against all reason, hoped.

When she didn't hear from Ted Parker all the next week she tried to persuade herself that he was out of town as he had said he might be.

Not all week, instinct told her. But she wouldn't listen to it.

That Saturday, glancing through the theater listings, the play at National Theater caught her eye. What if she bought two tickets to it, assuming they were available, called Ted Monday and said a friend had given them to her?

What night, though? (Oh God, what nights was Janet free next week? No use thinking of that.)

Thursday night? Yes, more of an off night than Friday.

She called the theater and was able to reserve two tickets for Thursday night's performance. "I'd like them mailed to me, please," she said. "I'll put a check in the mail today so that you'll have it Monday."

She called Ted Parker from home at eight-thirty Monday morning when he could usually be reached at his office before going out to the job site.

She spoke brightly when he came on the phone. "Hi Ted. It's Rita. Remember me?"

"Come on now," he said uncomfortably. "How've you been?"

"Just fine. And how are you?"

"They're keeping me very busy here these days."

"Are they? Not too busy, I hope, for something I have in mind."

"Well . . ."

Rita wouldn't let herself hear the wary note that came into his voice. She rushed on, "Someone gave a friend of mine two tickets for National Theater Thursday night. She can't use them and passed them on to me. I thought it might be fun for us to see it together if you're free. It's Eric Sykes and Jimmy Edwards in—"

"It sounds great, Rita, but I'm afraid I can't make it. I'll be tied up all Thursday evening. Thanks anyway, though, for thinking of me. I certainly appreciate it."

He was putting an end to the conversation. She couldn't

bring herself to suggest that she might be able to exchange the tickets for another night. That would be going down on her knees to him more than she had already.

"Well, just a thought I had." She kept her voice light. "Be seeing you."

"Yes, of course, we'll keep in touch. 'By for now."

"Good-by, Ted." She could barely hold back the sob in her throat until she hung up. Then, scorched with shame, she cried heartbrokenly, her head on the kitchen table.

She was half an hour late for work that morning. Make-up hid most of the ravages caused by her tears but Mrs. Wheelock realized that she had been through some sort of emotional storm the moment she came in the door.

Bob Sutton's interpretation of Rita's dead lost look and dragging step was that she'd had too big a weekend. He started to kid her about it but Mrs. Wheelock's frown silenced him.

She had made the coffee and after she had eased Sutton into his own office poured Rita a cup.

"Thank you," the latter said in a muffled voice taking the cover off her typewriter.

Mrs. Wheelock went back to her desk. The kindest thing to do was to let Rita alone until she was ready to talk about what was the matter.

The older woman did not doubt that it was connected with Ted Parker. As Rita had mentioned him less and less lately and the young glowing look left her face, it had become all too apparent that her happy interlude was over.

This morning she looked as old as time working by fits and starts, more often staring into space.

At noontime she said, "I don't feel like going to a restaurant today, Mrs. Wheelock. Will you settle for a sandwich at my house?"

"Of course."

And so, in the privacy of home, Rita poured out the whole story beginning with the night Janet met Ted Parker.

Once again she broke down and cried terribly, Mrs. Wheelock trying to offer what comfort she could.

No use thinking either how much she hated Janet for taking Ted away from her.

The evening turned out better than she had thought it would. They both enjoyed the show and discussing it afterward over supper at a restaurant nearby on Fourteenth Street.

Rita had driven her car. It was getting on toward midnight when she dropped Mrs. Wheelock off at her apartment telling her she hoped she would have a nice time tomorrow when she was taking the day off to spend it with an old friend who was passing through Washington.

Heading toward home on Route 7 Rita wasn't thinking about Ted Parker or might-have-beens until she had to stop for a red light and realized that the street on her right led to Janet's apartment.

Her loss came flooding back. Tied up all Thursday evening Ted Parker had told her. Tied up with Janet?

As the light changed to green her car, almost of its own volition, it seemed, took the right turn toward Janet's.

The second right after that, wasn't it? But what was the point in going there? Janet would be in bed unless she was still out somewhere or working the night shift at the hospital.

Rita reached the apartment complex and turned into the parking lot close to Janet's entrance.

A light shone through the drawn venetian blind on her front window. It didn't necessarily mean she was home, Rita reminded herself. She could have gone out and left the light on.

There was no point in staying just as there had been no point in coming at all.

As Rita backed her car around to leave her headlights picked up Janet's red Vega parked a few slots beyond the entrance to her apartment. She was home apparently or at least not out anywhere in her own car.

Rita drove to the end of the parking area to circle back onto the street. The last car in it was Ted Parker's new green Chevrolet.

The shock of it—afterward she would ask herself why it

It was two o'clock before they got back to the offi
matter. Young, as usual, was gone for the day and
off somewhere.

When the afternoon was over and they were gettir
close up the office Mrs. Wheelock said, "Rita, why
come to my place for dinner and spend the night?"

"Oh, that's not necessary. I'll be all right."

"I've got chops in the refrigerator and you know
keep my guest room bed made up. In fact," Mrs. V
paused and added with mock sternness, "if you don't c
land on your doorstep tonight and how will you like tl
sure you're not in the mood for entertaining company."

Rita laughed, a weak laugh but the first one that da
really," she said.

"Well then, that settles it. You run home and pick up
ever you'll need and I'll go on ahead to my place and get
organized."

Rita protested no more. The last thing she wanted was
home alone tonight.

Instead, the evening passed pleasantly. They had two di
before dinner and afterward talked about all sorts of th
that had no connection with Ted Parker. At bedtime I
Wheelock made them each a nightcap, Rita's much stron
than it would have been ordinarily.

"So you'll sleep," the older woman said. "Tomorrow's
other day, Rita, and life goes on."

Between the nightcap and her own exhaustion, Rita slej
soundly that night in Mrs. Wheelock's guest room and looke
much better at breakfast the next morning.

"Those theater tickets will be in the mail today," she said
"They shouldn't go to waste. Shall we see the show togethei
Thursday night, Mrs. Wheelock?"

"Love to. And we'll go somewhere afterward for supper."

Getting dressed for the theater Thursday night Rita didn't
let herself dwell on how different she had hoped it would be;
Ted Parker picking her up, the evening a great success, they
back on the old footing, Janet forgotten.

should have been a shock—made her stall her motor. Perversely then, it wouldn't start, no matter how frantically she pressed down on the starter. Too frantically, she realized and forced herself to sit back and wait a few moments before she tried again.

All she could think of while she waited was the humiliation she would suffer if Ted Parker came out of Janet's apartment just then on his way home.

The next time her foot touched the starter the motor caught. She drove off as fast as she could, promising herself that she would never go back there again.

When she had calmed down from what she kept thinking of as a narrow escape she was free to torment herself with thoughts of the phone call she had made Monday.

Tied up all Thursday evening. . . . The words haunted her.

Oh God, how she hated Janet. Ted Parker too.

But most of all herself who had somehow, somehow lost the way long ago back in her childhood.

Back in Dolly's time.

IX

Rita couldn't believe it at first; it couldn't be happening to her that she had to face Janet here in a restaurant at 7 Corners shopping center only two days after she had seen Ted Parker's car at Janet's apartment house. It was too much; she just couldn't take it.

But she had no choice. Smiling, waving, Janet followed in the hostess's wake to the table where Rita sat alone.

"Hi Rita," she said cheerfully settling into the chair the hostess drew out and picking up the menu laid in front of her. "This is a break for me. Such a big Saturday crowd I thought I'd have to wait for a table or sit with some stranger but then I spotted you and said you were a friend I could join."

A friend, thought Rita. A friend.

"How've you been?" Janet continued. "Haven't seen you since the night at your house. Keeping busy?"

"Pretty much." Wasn't there malice in the tone, the gaze fixed on Rita? "How about you?"

Janet giggled. "Seems as if I'm on the go all the time. In fact, I'm here at 7 Corners now to look for a dress to wear to the theater tonight. The National to see—well, I forget the name of the show. Have you seen it?"

"Yes." Had Ted told Janet that Rita had asked him to go with her? No, he couldn't have done that. It would be too mean.

But there was that malice in the big brown eyes. Wouldn't it be there anyway, though, with Janet reveling to herself in the knowledge that she had taken Ted away from Rita?

"Did you enjoy it?"

"Oh yes. So did the man I saw it with. Is Sam Richards taking you?" Rita couldn't hold the question back.

"No, someone else."

Ted, of course. It might well be that it was Rita's invitation to him that had led to his asking Janet to go.

The waitress took Janet's order.

Rita felt trapped. Having just started her own lunch, there would be no quick escape for her. She had to go on acting as if nothing had changed.

"Seen Ted Parker lately?" Janet asked.

That was really twisting the knife.

If you knew how I hate you, thought Rita as she replied, "Not since we had dinner together a week or more ago."

Score one for her. Janet's eyes flickered. She hadn't known about it. No reason Ted should have mentioned it to her. He wouldn't be apt to bring up Rita at all. Which meant that he wouldn't have mentioned her theater invitation either.

There was some comfort in that thought even though it gave her a fresh pang of sorrow over losing him.

When Janet's order was served Rita asked for her check.

"What's your hurry?" Janet inquired picking up her fork.

"Well, I've finished my shopping and I want to take advantage of a nice day like this to start on some clean-up work in my yard."

"Not my kind of thing ever," said Janet. "Or taking care of a house either. Especially one that's practically out in the country. Don't you get nervous at night sometimes there alone?"

"No, I like it. I'd feel cooped up in an apartment like yours."

Janet shrugged. "Well, if you're satisfied, that's what counts. If I were in your shoes, though, I'd at least want a roommate. The money as well as the company. But come to think of it, you have had roommates in the past, haven't you?"

"Yes." Rita chewed and swallowed steadily. She could leave

a little on her plate but not too much, not enough to make Janet think she was trying to get away from her.

"Oh, that reminds me—" Janet gave her an innocent look. "One of the nurses at the hospital is a friend of your last roommate, Louise—I don't recall her last name."

"Brooks." Dear God, did it have to be such a small world?

The things Louise must have said about her. "Regular old maid, the fuss she makes over her house. Hardly ever had any dates and resented it that I had so many. You can't imagine the scene she made because I had a chance to go to Kennedy Center instead of a movie with her. I got out the next day. I'd had all I could take of her. . . ."

Louise had said things like that to her friend the nurse who had passed them on to Janet.

Wasn't it bad enough that she could gloat over Ted without having Louise to gloat over too?

Rita couldn't bring herself to look at Janet just then and kept her eyes on her plate.

"I guess it isn't always easy to find a congenial roommate," Janet said next. "You haven't had much luck so far, it seems, so perhaps it is better for you to live by yourself, no matter how lonely it is at times."

Rita read between the lines: You can't keep a man; you can't even keep a roommate. What a loser you are.

She forced her gaze up to the smiling pretty face across the table with the innocent expression still on it.

Suddenly she couldn't bear the role assigned to her and heard herself say, "As a matter of fact, I have a new roommate moving in shortly. A very attractive girl too."

"Oh." Janet sounded taken aback. "What's her name?"

It came to Rita spontaneously. "Winifred."

"What's her last name?"

"Lawton." Where did that come from? "Winifred Lawton."

"What does she do?"

"She's—" Rita's glance fell on the hostess seating people at the next table—"a hostess. In a cocktail lounge."

"In Washington or around here?"

"Well, what a cross-examination!" Rita's suppressed pain, her hatred of Janet, threatened to break out in her tone.

"Sorry." Janet's shrug expressed amusement. "Didn't know it was a secret."

"It isn't." Rita fished a name out of her memory. "The Blue Grotto on K Street."

"The Blue Grotto?" Janet was impressed. She had never been there herself but had heard it mentioned at the hospital as a very plush place to go.

"How old is Winifred?"

"Around my age. She's been married and divorced." That added a special flair, Rita thought.

"Winifred Lawton," Janet said reflectively. "I don't think I've ever heard you mention her. Have you known her long?"

"Heaven's sake, Janet, I haven't told you my whole life story." Rita finished her coffee and pushed back her chair. "I really must be going. Have a nice time tonight."

Janet smiled, once more in ascendancy. "I'm sure I will." She added with a final touch of malice, "Have a nice time yourself, Rita, working in your yard."

She made gardening sound like the dullest thing possible that anyone could do on a Saturday afternoon. Even so, Rita still felt a small sense of one-upmanship as she left. At least Janet would have to stop thinking that no one would come to live with her. Winifred Lawton, attractive divorcee, cocktail hostess at The Blue Grotto, put Louise Brooks in the shade.

Also, Janet could be relied upon to carry the story back to the nurse at the hospital and she, in turn, would pass it on to Louise Brooks.

There'd be no way for them to check on it. Rita didn't know the nurse and had no intention of ever seeing Janet or Louise again except for a chance meeting like today's.

On the way to her car a display of party dresses in a store window caught her eye. Had Janet seen them yet? She would look lovely in one of them going to the theater tonight.

Going with Ted. But that was too hurtful to think about.

Instead, concentrating on the dresses, the thought came to

her that Winifred Lawton, cocktail hostess, would look lovely in one of them too. . . .

The last thing Rita was prepared for Monday morning was any reference to Winifred.

But Mrs. Wheelock brought her name up while the coffee was perking.

"Well, Rita, so you've found a new roommate," she said. "It was quite a surprise when I heard about it."

Rita, getting out the cups, almost dropped one.

"You've seen Janet," she said after a moment.

"Yes. I ran into her Saturday afternoon at 7 Corners."

Of course, thought Rita. They both lived in Falls Church with 7 Corners conveniently nearby. Nothing unusual at all for them to run into each other there.

Except that it had never entered Rita's mind that they would; that the story she had made up on the spur of the moment would immediately turn into chickens come home to roost.

"It must have been quite a surprise," Rita said stalling for time. "What did you say to Janet?"

"As little as I could. I certainly wasn't going to say it was news to me. After all that she's done, she isn't exactly one of my favorite people, you know."

Rita felt a surge of affection for the older woman who was so kind and motherly toward her, so clearly on her side.

She was close to telling her the truth about Winifred at that moment; but Bob Sutton arrived just then and the subject was dropped while they all had coffee together.

With this interlude for further reflection, Rita realized that she didn't want to admit she had invented the Winifred story, goaded into it by Janet. Mrs. Wheelock, regardless of how fond she was of Rita, would be bound to see her as a forlorn figure in it.

There was pride to be redeemed too after the way Rita had gone to pieces in front of her last week over Ted. Pride could mean not only naked to one's enemies but naked to one's friends as well.

Even as she told herself all this, however, Rita knew that part of the reason for her unwillingness to reveal the true story was that she liked her concept of Winifred and did not want to relinquish it so quickly.

There would be time enough for it later, for saying Winifred had found a place of her own or was giving up her job or something of the sort. There would be plenty of ways to let her go.

The immediate problem was what to tell Mrs. Wheelock. She couldn't just say Winifred was a friend of hers as she had with Janet. Mrs. Wheelock had either met or heard of everyone in her relatively small circle of friends. What could she tell her?

Rita turned this question over in her mind while the older woman was in Gene Young's office. By the time their regular morning conference was over she had her story ready.

She related it after the two men had left. "I met her Friday," she began. "I felt like going somewhere different for lunch since you weren't here and went to that delicatessen we like in Alexandria. It was so crowded they seated me with a girl who was by herself."

"Winifred?"

"Yes. Winifred Lawton. While we were waiting to be served we got into a conversation that was very friendly and relaxed. You know how I am—not too quick to take up with strangers— but before lunch was over I began to feel as if I'd known Winifred all my life."

"Heavens, you really were taken with her. How old is she?"

"Oh, around thirty maybe. Anyway, during lunch—I ordered one of those marvelous corned beef sandwiches you always get (Now why did she have to embroider on the story like that?)— she told me she was looking for someone to share an apartment with and how hard it was to find the right person."

"Where is she living now?"

"Temporarily, with a married couple, friends of hers, in Washington."

"Doesn't she have her own furniture?"

"Some, I gathered, but it's stored at her mother's in upstate

New York. She mentioned the town but I've forgotten the name of it. She's divorced—quite recently from what she said."

"Has she got a job?"

"She's just taken one as a cocktail hostess at The Blue Grotto on K Street."

Like Janet, Mrs. Wheelock had heard of it but had never been there. Unlike Janet, however, she was not impressed with a good-looking divorcee working as a hostess in a fashionable restaurant; someone from out-of-state too with what seemed like vague antecedents. Her gaze rested thoughtfully on Rita. "You said she could move in with you?"

"Oh no, nothing as firm as that, if that's what Janet told you. It's just that my house came into the conversation and that I'd had a roommate who left soon after New Year's."

"And she was interested?"

"She seemed to be. She's coming to see me tonight after work. She works all sorts of different hours."

(Why did she keep getting herself deeper and deeper into this? And what would Mrs. Wheelock think of her if she knew Rita was making the whole thing up?)

"Well, that sounds a little better," Mrs. Wheelock said. "From what Janet said, I thought it was all cut and dried. What did you say Winifred's last name was?"

"Lawton."

"Oh yes. Winifred Lawton. I guess I've got it straight now. But I must say I was in a state of total confusion, racking my brain to think who she could be when Janet started telling me about her."

"I can imagine."

"Still, it won't hurt to take plenty of time over this, Rita. After all, she is a perfect stranger to you—"

"Winifred?" Rita's voice went flat. "I don't feel that she is. I feel as if I've always known her."

"Even so—"

Rita's momentary resentment vanished with the realization that she had to keep a line of retreat open on Winifred.

"Don't worry," she said. "We'll talk tonight but nothing will be decided."

Her phone rang just then. The call involved a discussion with Mrs. Wheelock and after that nothing more was said about Winifred. Rita knew, however, that fairly soon she would have to tell the older woman that she had thought better of letting Winifred come to live with her.

But not just yet.

Mrs. Wheelock, still a little concerned about it, aware of how particularly vulnerable Rita was to any new relationship right now after what had happened with Ted Parker, called her that night around quarter of ten.

"Did Winifred come?" she asked.

"Oh yes. She got here at eight and stayed about an hour. I showed her through the house and she liked the room she would have. It was all very pleasant but nothing was settled. She wants to be careful too, I guess. Anyway, we're going to have dinner together some night soon and talk about it again."

Mrs. Wheelock expressed approval of this go-slow approach and after she had hung up reflected that unhappy as Rita was right now, Winifred might, after all, turn out to be the best thing that could happen to her. A point in Winifred's favor was that she didn't seem prepared to make any hasty decision on their living together.

But Mrs. Wheelock still had misgivings about the situation. It was Rita's quickness in reaching out to Winifred that gave them to her. Which one had suggested having dinner together soon? Rita, probably, forcing the pace with Winifred just as she had with Ted Parker.

Wasn't she ever going to learn from experience? Apparently not.

Rita, after talking with Mrs. Wheelock, found herself listening to the quiet of the house. It would be nice, she thought, to have someone else there to break in on it. Someone like Winifred.

What did Winifred look like?

That was a stupid thought. Winifred didn't exist.

But when she went upstairs to bed she stood in the doorway of the empty room across the hall from hers. It would be Winifred's room—if there were a Winifred.

It was a pretty room, well-furnished, in perfect order like the rest of the house. And just as quiet.

It needed a Winifred to bring it to life.

There was no Winifred. No Ted. No one at all.

Rita fled to her own room and suddenly began to cry.

X

Tuesday brought Easter weekend one day closer. Rita thought about it at breakfast and shrank from the prospect of spending it in Granville with her parents. It was more than she could face just now, so soon after what had happened with Ted. On the other hand, it would be rather dreary to be here alone the whole three days.

That part of the problem was solved Tuesday night. A cousin, recently moved to Leesburg, called and asked Rita to have Easter dinner with her and her husband.

Rita accepted the invitation and then phoned her mother. She might have to work Friday, she said, and anyway, Easter came so early this year she could count on better weather if she postponed her visit for a couple of weeks. Easter Sunday? The cousin in Leesburg took care of that.

"Well, it's nice she asked you," Rita's mother said. "And as long as you're not coming, your father and I may have dinner at the Gleasons'. You've heard me speak of them. The wife is in my bridge club."

"Yes, I remember," said Rita.

Her mother, she thought as she hung up, was probably just as pleased that she wasn't coming as she was not to go.

But still, it made her feel more left out than ever that her mother had alternative plans and had voiced no great disappointment that she wouldn't be with them that weekend.

The rest of the week passed uneventfully. Rita bowled Wednesday night. Friday night she played bridge at the

Hunts's, the fourth player a widower who had been her partner several times before.

Driving home at midnight it occurred to her that she had not mentioned where she was going that night to Mrs. Wheelock. There was no reason, therefore, that she couldn't tell her Monday that Winifred had called her tonight right after she got home, that they had gone out to dinner together and had a lovely time. However, she could add, they still hadn't reached a decision on becoming roommates.

Why not? Well, it more or less depended on Winifred's job. She wanted to be sure she liked it before making any long-range plans.

The story sounded perfectly plausible, Rita thought, and gave her an out for dropping Winifred from her life a little later on.

But not just yet.

When she was almost home, though, she began to feel uneasy, not for the first time, over what she was doing. It wasn't so much that she was involving herself in so many lies—hadn't she become an accomplished liar long ago over Dolly?—but because she couldn't seem to put the idea of Winifred out of her life once and for all as she really should.

It would be easy enough to do it. Just say to Mrs. Wheelock that Winifred had told her tonight that she wasn't too happy with her job; that she had been thinking all week about giving it up and returning to her mother's in New York State; and that until she reached a decision, the question of where she would live was left up in the air.

That was the story she should tell Mrs. Wheelock Monday morning.

But she didn't want to do that. She wanted to keep Winifred a little longer.

Why? she asked herself turning in at her driveway.

She didn't really know. It was just that—well, in a sense, Winifred was company for her.

But that was too silly for words. Worse than that. Crazy. If she didn't watch out, next thing she knew, she would begin thinking of Winifred as a real person.

No, she wouldn't, she assured herself crossing the yard to her back door. Not as long as she realized it was all just a game—something that made her feel less alone, even comforted her a little over losing Ted who was—be honest with herself, face the stark truth for a moment—not just the man she had started to build dreams around on short acquaintance but also a symbol of other men she had lost out with in the past.

When Rita was ready for bed, she went into the other bedroom—Winifred's room, if she existed—and turned on the light.

She opened the closet door. Not much in it except a few old clothes she had hung there after Louise moved out. She had been meaning to get rid of them as well as the hatboxes on the shelf. How long since she had last worn a hat? She really should clear the closet out.

Her glance fell on the bare polished top of the bureau. It needed something on it. One of Aunt Edna's bureau scarfs? She went out to the linen closet in the hall and picked out the nicest one she could find, raw silk with a delicate embroidered edging, half laughing, half chiding herself over what she was doing but still picking out the nicest one.

It dressed the old cherry bureau up, she thought, centering it carefully and standing back to view the effect. It was too fragile for everyday use but here in Winifred's room that didn't matter.

Winifred's room.

Rita looked at herself in the mirror. "You'd better cut this out," she told her reflection and turned out the light and went to bed.

But Saturday afternoon found her upstairs in the storage space that ran across the back of the house getting out a box of ornaments that had belonged to her great-aunt. A small round bowl of hand-painted china, old-fashioned but pretty, looked rather nice on the bureau. A silver-mounted hand mirror black with tarnish was her next find. She took it downstairs and polished it before she placed it near the bowl. A delft blue candlestick with a white candle in it added another touch.

The nightstand by the bed caught her eye. That should have something on it too besides the reading lamp already there. A clock? If it really were Winifred's room she would have an electric alarm clock. Hadn't Louise left an old one in the storage space?

Rita located it, set the time and plugged it in.

The box yielded a white ceramic kitten, too plump and curlicued for modern taste but quaint enough to furbish up the nightstand.

The spinet desk came next. She had put a fresh sheet of blotting paper in the desk pad after Louise moved out but the pigeonholes had nothing in them.

She went down to the secretary in the living room for paper, envelopes, pencils and pens. In the back of a drawer she came upon her aunt Edna's heavy silver paper knife that she never used herself, polished it and took it upstairs with the rest.

The empty pigeonholes filled up. The paper knife gleamed against the pale yellow blotting paper. A rush-bottomed chair, placed at an angle in front of the desk made it look as if Winifred had just got up from writing a letter.

Rita surveyed the room from the doorway. It looked much more inviting, more lived-in.

Before she left for Easter dinner in Leesburg the next day she cleared out the closet in the room, packing the old clothes and hats in cartons to take to the Salvation Army.

One of the dresses, a pale green print, brought her up short as she slipped it off the hanger. How odd that all the years she'd had it she had never noticed before that it was the same shade of green with a similar print to the dress Dolly had put on that day.

Their mother's dress, almost brand-new, taken from her closet.

Rita aghast at her daring. Don't, Dolly, put it back! Mama'll have a fit if she catches you.

But Dolly, who had fallen in love with the dress the day

their mother bought it, just laughed and held it up in front of her trailing on the floor while Rita rummaged through their dress-up box for what she would wear.

Dolly was quick to laugh off warnings about getting caught and charming in penitence when it happened.

All quicksilver charm, that was Dolly.

If she had lived, she would have been twenty-seven years old next month, two years younger than Rita.

How would her life have turned out?

She would be married, of course. Happily married, too, being Dolly. She would have children who adored her just as everyone had during her short lifetime. Little pixies probably, like herself.

That was what Aunt Edna used to call her. . . .

Dolly had rolled their mother's green dress up that day and put it in the big pocketbook with their play money, Rita still upset over it, saying she would get blamed too because she was supposed to set a good example.

Their mother was canning in the kitchen as she had been all day. Rita called to her from the front hall that they were going to play outdoors and she said all right.

Wobbling in their mother's old high-heeled shoes, they had to cross two fields with a fence between to reach their destination, an abandoned railroad trestle over a wooded ravine.

The Nancy Drew books had come into their lives that summer. Dolly couldn't read yet but Rita sometimes read them aloud to her. The books had led to a game she had invented recently, centering on their play money and the railroad trestle.

Dolly waited until after she had climbed the fence to put on the green dress over her shorts and jersey and then had to bunch the dress up so as not to trip over it.

The guilt, the horror of it, the deep wound left that had never quite healed . . .

Only a few months past eight years old herself at the time and scared to death. Even so, what would another eight-year-old have done?

All the years since that question had stayed in her mind.

What good did it do to ask it again?

Rita packed the green dress and covered it quickly with other things to get it out of sight.

When she was finished, cartons sealed up, the closet was empty.

She was ready then to leave for Leesburg.

After dinner that afternoon her cousin brought out her wedding album and a collection of snapshots taken at the reception by various guests. Rita herself appeared in a few of them but the one that interested her the most was of a handsome auburn-haired woman about thirty years old. She stood alone in the doorway to the club lounge. She was wearing a deep blue dress of some silky fabric and jewelry that set it off. Her eyes were bright blue. She was smiling slightly as if amused at being asked to pose for her picture.

"Who's that?" Rita asked her cousin. "I don't remember seeing her at your wedding. She's very elegant-looking."

"If you hadn't asked me her name I could have told you what it was," the cousin replied. "Now it's gone clear out of my head. She lives in Charleston. Her husband has some sort of business connection with my father-in-law."

"I don't see how I could have missed her, anyone as striking as that."

"Well, you could have easily because, as I recall it, she didn't stay very long. She and her husband were going on to some other affair. And there were, after all, around one hundred and fifty people at my wedding."

Rita's cousin put the picture aside with others already looked at and produced a fresh assortment. Presently, however, the phone rang and she left the room to answer it.

While she was gone Rita went back through the pile and got out the woman's picture again.

Who did she remind her of?

No one, really. But still—

At last it came to her. This was what Winifred would look like with the same sophisticated style and good looks. The Blue

Grotto probably had cocktail hostesses like her, this handsome woman whose name she didn't know.

It could be Winifred. If Winifred existed. Even though she didn't, at least Rita now knew what she would look like if she did.

There must be some way she could keep the picture.

When her cousin returned Rita held it up and said, "I've been looking at this again because it just dawned on me that the woman is the image of a friend of mine in Washington. They're practically doubles. Would you mind if I borrowed it to show to her?"

"Of course not. Let her keep it if she wants to. It's certainly not very important to me when I can't even remember the woman's name."

"Thank you." Rita put it in her pocketbook.

When she got home that night she took it into the other bedroom and stood it up against the mirror.

Find a frame for it? No. Winifred—if she existed—wouldn't frame a picture of herself and put it on her bureau. Something more casual was called for.

Rita slid the picture in between the mirror and the frame. Anyone might do that with a favorite snapshot of themselves.

It added a personal touch, almost gave substance to Winifred.

Almost was the key word in her thought. She mustn't take this Winifred business too seriously.

But there was no harm in it as long as it was just a game.

XI

Rita made her postponed trip to Granville the second weekend after Easter.

The Tuesday before her trip she received a letter from her mother that included mention of a call from Mrs. Murray who told her that Janet hadn't got home for Easter either but was expected some weekend soon.

"It better not be this weekend," Rita declared the next day to Mrs. Wheelock. "If she calls me asking for a ride I won't even make up an excuse for not taking her. I'll just say it's more convenient to go by myself."

But there was no call from Janet that would put her to the test of a flat refusal.

"She must be going some other weekend," Rita said Friday morning. "She would never drive herself if she thought she could get a free ride with me."

Mrs. Wheelock nodded and changed the subject, troubled by the bitterness in Rita's tone. She wanted to tell her that nursing her hatred of Janet would do more damage to her than to Janet herself but could think of no way to get her to accept that, at least not yet.

They left work early that afternoon, Rita driving Mrs. Wheelock to National Airport before setting out for Granville.

"I'll miss you," she said, helping her get her luggage out of the car at the main terminal building. The older woman was taking a week's vacation, staying overnight with her sister in

New York and then flying to Idaho to visit her son and his family.

"Well, I should hope so," Mrs. Wheelock replied briskly. "I wouldn't want you to spend all next week congratulating yourself on not having me around."

Rita laughed but still felt a small sense of loss as they said good-by.

She reached Granville a little earlier that night than on her last trip when she'd had Janet with her. After the slight bustle of her arrival she unpacked and presented her Easter gifts, perfume for her mother, a leather tobacco pouch for her father. In return they gave her a check for twenty-five dollars.

"We didn't know what to get you," her mother said.

It was a superfluous remark. They always gave her a check for Easter, her birthday and Christmas. Writing a check was easier than trying to think of some gift-wrapped package she would enjoy opening.

Actually, Rita reminded herself, she preferred the check. Even so—

As they sat talking in the living room she learned that her aunt had invited them to dinner tomorrow night and that Sunday her aunt and uncle would be coming here.

"Ham," her mother said. "I got a real nice one. I'll plan dinner for one o'clock so that you'll get an early start driving back."

Sunday dinner served at one o'clock went as far back as Rita could remember. It was another thing that never changed in this house.

She went to bed before eleven o'clock saying she was tired from her drive. Her parents soon followed her upstairs.

All day tomorrow had to be filled in, she thought, wakeful in her familiar yet alien room. Then it would be Sunday and she could leave right after dinner.

Tomorrow, though, would last forever. . . .

But it turned out to be not as bad as Rita had feared. She slept until nine, made her own breakfast while her mother followed her usual routine of morning chores and her father read the paper.

Then he asked if she would drive him downtown to pick up his car at a garage where he was having some work done on it. That took up time. After lunch he had to take her mother, who had never learned to drive, to the hairdresser.

"I hope you don't mind being left here alone," her mother said. "I never gave it a thought that you'd be here this weekend when I made the appointment and then it was too late to change it."

"That's all right, Mama," Rita replied. "I brought a book along and I'll settle down and read or perhaps take a walk."

"Well, if that's the case," her father said, "I'll putter around downtown and wait for your mother. I usually do that when she has a hair appointment so as not to have to go back and get her."

Rita lingered on the back porch after their departure. The day was cool but pleasant inviting her outdoors. But as she went upstairs to get her sweater she changed her mind about taking a walk. It would only lead her toward the railroad trestle where she had no desire to go; and her parents' absence removed the need to get out of the house herself.

She got her book and then hesitated in the doorway to her room. She didn't really feel much like reading just now.

She was facing the attic door. How long since she had been up there? Four or five years ago. Aunt Edna was still alive at the time and during a weekend visit her mother had sent her up to look for some family picture or other that Aunt Edna wanted to see.

Rita put her book down and went up into the attic.

At the top of the stairs she stood looking around her. Nothing had changed here either. The same discarded pieces of furniture were lined up along the walls, interspersed with boxes and cartons labeled in her mother's neat precise handwriting. The cedar chest occupied the same space under the front window with the trunk that held Dolly's clothes next to it.

It was a large trunk as it had to be to hold all of them. The only ones not in it were the bloodstained shorts and jersey Dolly was wearing under the green dress that day.

After a moment Rita went over to the trunk and raised the lid, wrinkling her nose at the strong smell of mothballs that came from it.

Winter coat, snowsuit, spring coat, sweaters, dresses, overalls, jumpers, blouses, pajamas, robes, underwear, shoes, mittens, hats— Her mother should have got rid of them long ago, Rita thought impatiently, careful not to disturb their order as she looked at them; or rather, they should never have been kept in the first place. Some sort of masochistic streak in her mother had led to this morbid clinging to the past.

She had that same streak in herself, she knew.

It surfaced when she came upon a blue plaid dress with a yoked front. She took it out and spread it over the edge of the trunk. Nothing else in it could strike a more painful chord in her memory.

She was starting third grade that September, Dolly first. Their mother had taken them shopping just before school opened, buying them new shoes and a new dress, a red plaid for Rita and the blue plaid for Dolly.

They had worn their new dresses the first day of school and once or twice more before Dolly died. Then Dolly's was laundered and packed away with the rest of her clothes.

Rita, arriving home from school the week after the funeral, found her mother in the kitchen ironing them.

"Are you going to give them to someone, Mama?" she ventured to ask.

"No."

"Then why—? Dolly won't be wearing them anymore."

"I know." Her mother, lips pressed together, gave Rita a remote look. "But I want them to look just so when I put them away."

That night, for the first time in her life, Rita walked in her sleep and continued to do so now and then for months thereafter. It was almost a year before her sleepwalking gradually came to an end.

Rita didn't want to think about any of that now and turned away from the trunk quickly.

But she wasn't ready to go downstairs yet. She wandered around looking at the labels on cartons and boxes pausing in front of one that said "Dolly's toys" without looking inside it.

She shook her head over two cartons labeled "Aluminum Cookware." Why hadn't that been given away when her mother replaced it with stainless steel? What a pack rat she was!

Rita halted next in front of a box labeled "Pictures" and opened it, the same box her mother had sent her up to look through when she was there with Aunt Edna.

It had not been opened since, apparently, because on top of the pile was her aunt Mary and uncle Roger's wedding picture in color, the one, she now recalled, that she had been sent up to find.

They made an attractive couple, Rita thought. Aunt Mary's wedding dress, in the style of 1940, was really quite pretty.

She pulled out the tab on the easelback of the gold-leaf frame and stood it up to catch the light.

Aunt Mary had the same pale red hair as Rita's father. It was nowhere near the deep auburn of Winifred's—the unknown woman's hair—but it was red.

Why not take the picture home with her? It would never be missed and would look nice on the bureau in the other room.

What about the box of ornaments she had passed over? She might find something she could use in it.

Rita opened it. Most of what it held was of no interest to her until she came upon the mate to the silly curlicued kitten she had found in Aunt Edna's box of ornaments. Aunt Edna's stood on its four legs; this one was rolled up into a ball. They had once been a pair, whoever they had belonged to originally; she would take this one home and unite them once again.

The only other find she made was an old cut-glass scent bottle.

She hadn't realized how much time she had spent in the attic until she heard her father's car drive in.

She closed the trunk, gathered up the things she was taking with her, and hurried down the attic stairs to get them out of sight in her suitcase before her parents came into the house.

Then it occurred to her that she would feel more comfortable if she locked her suitcase. Not that her mother would have any reason to open it but still, she would feel more comfortable with it locked.

When she had done this and put the key in her pocketbook she was ready to go downstairs. Her watch said quarter of four. They would set out for her aunt Mary's around five-thirty. Dinner there was served at six o'clock just as it was here.

Meanwhile, with less than twenty-four hours of her visit remaining, the evening paper would help to pass the time. And tomorrow, right after dinner, she would be free to leave.

When Rita arrived home Sunday night and had brought in her mail and the newspapers, she took her suitcase upstairs and unpacked it.

The things she had brought from the attic went straight across the hall into the other room.

"There," she said aloud to the kitten putting it on the nightstand beside its mate, "you're back together again. I wonder how many years you've been apart. Even though you're a couple of Victorian horrors, you do look sort of cute, the two of you smirking at each other."

The wedding picture involved some rearrangement of the bureau to get a balanced effect. Aunt Mary and Uncle Roger could be taken for Winifred's—the unknown woman's—parents considering that Aunt Mary had red hair too.

Rita herself had no picture of her parents on display. But then, she had never been as close to them as Winifred—if she existed—would probably have been to hers.

The cut-glass bottle looked cloudy. It had better have a good soaking with ammonia in the water before Rita put any of her own cologne in it.

She left the closet door open to air it out. She would give it a good cleaning tomorrow night after work. There would really be nothing left to do then in the room except to get the scent bottle bright and sparkling again.

XII

The week flew by. With Mrs. Wheelock away, Rita was kept so busy at the office that she scarcely had time to miss her. Wednesday night she bowled and Thursday night went out to dinner with the Hunts and their widower neighbor. She did her grocery shopping on her way home from work Friday night and put a load in the washer before she started getting dinner ready.

She was folding clean laundry when the doorbell rang a little after eight o'clock. It was Janet who stood on the doorstep with Rita's coffee pot in her hand.

"Hi," she said gaily holding it out. "Did you think I was never going to bring it back?"

"I didn't think about it at all." Rita took it from her. "Uh— won't you come in?"

She had no choice on that with Janet already over the threshold.

"I wasn't doing anything tonight so I thought I might as well return it and if you weren't home leave it at the door or something."

As Janet was speaking she moved ahead of Rita into the living room and without being asked dropped down in a chair. "How've you been? Haven't seen you for ages."

"Just fine." Rita sat down herself reluctantly.

"I hear you didn't go home for Easter. Neither did I. I was on night duty all that weekend."

Not out with Ted then. Was she still seeing him?

No way to find out short of asking. And Rita would rather die than do that.

Janet had a question of her own. "Where's your roommate? I've forgotten her name—"

Of course she hadn't. Curiosity about Winifred, not returning the coffee pot, was what had really brought her here tonight.

"Winifred Lawton."

"Oh yes. Is she at The Blue Grotto tonight?"

"No, she's away for the weekend."

"Too bad. I'd like to have met her."

"Well, she won't be back until late Sunday night."

"She must be all settled in by this time."

"Yes."

"How're you getting on together?"

"Just fine."

"That's good. Keeps you from being alone too much."

One of Janet's sly digs, Rita thought. "Oh, I don't know about that," she replied crisply. "I keep busy with or without Winifred and so does she. We don't really see all that much of each other."

"Is that so? Just as well, I guess. Doesn't pay to get too dependent on anyone."

That was another dig, wasn't it? But the pretty face showed only blandness. Then Janet added plaintively, "Aren't you going to offer me a drink, Rita?"

"Oh, sorry." Rita got up and went out into the kitchen to make drinks for them. There would be no offer of a second one, though, she told herself. All she wanted was for Janet to leave.

But Janet seemed in no hurry to do that, sipping her drink, regaling Rita with details of places she had been, how much in demand she was.

The most galling part of having to sit and listen to it was the knowledge that it was mainly true. Janet probably had more dates in a month than Rita had in a year. Including, these days, dates with Ted Parker.

It would have been no comfort to Rita if Janet had told her he had gone back to his home office and would be away for several weeks.

Presently Janet reverted to the subject that had brought her there.

"Is Winifred as neat and organized as you are, Rita?"

"Yes." Rita's tone was curt with the anger festering inside her.

"Well then, no problems in that department."

Still another dig, Rita realized, based on the stories Louis Brooks had passed on.

Janet finished her drink. When no refill was offered she said, "I guess I'd better be running along now," and stood up to leave. "May I use your bathroom first, though?"

"Yes. You know where it is." Rita's tone was still curt but as Janet started upstairs it occurred to her that what she really wanted was a chance to look over Winifred's room.

To forestall that, Rita scooped up an armload of clean laundry and hurried up the stairs after her.

When Janet emerged from the bathroom she was at the linen closet in the hall putting away towels. Even so, Janet halted in the doorway of the other room, switched on the light and glanced around it. "My, Winifred is neat, isn't she? Everything in its place."

She sauntered over to the bureau. "Is that her parents' wedding picture?"

"Yes." Rita was close at her heels.

"How odd to keep something as dated as that on display. You'd think she'd want something more recent."

She was right, of course. Rita should have looked for an older couple while going through the pictures in the attic. On the other hand, it was none of Janet's business if Winifred chose to keep her parents' wedding picture on her bureau.

"Is this Winifred?" Janet took the snapshot out of the mirror.

"Yes."

"Why, she's stunning, Rita. Sort of—well, sophisticated-looking. You didn't tell me that about her."

"Didn't I?" Satisfaction surged in Rita that she had gained status in Janet's eyes.

"Her dress is stunning too. Let's see the rest of her clothes." Janet put the snapshot back and turned toward the closet.

But Rita was ahead of her backing up against the closet door.

"Indeed not," she said sharply. "I wouldn't think of snooping through her belongings myself and certainly wouldn't let anyone else do it."

"Oh well, if that's the way you feel—" Janet shrugged and reversed direction toward the hall saying over her shoulder, "I think you're being a bit silly, though, Rita. What harm in looking at Winifred's clothes?"

"None, maybe, but everyone has a right to their privacy."

"Have it your way." Janet went downstairs with Rita right behind her. As she picked up her pocketbook in the living room she said sweetly, "When I do get to meet Winifred, I'll tell her what a stern protector you are of her rights, Rita." She giggled. "You should have seen yourself up there flat against the closet door, looking like you were guarding the gold at Fort Knox. I swear you would have knocked me down if I had tried to get past you."

"I might have," Rita answered unsmilingly and opened the front door for Janet. "Good night," she said. "Thanks for bringing back my coffee pot."

"I should have returned it long ago but better late than never. Oh, did I thank you for the drink?" There was stress laid on the noun singular.

"You're welcome."

Rita stood in the doorway until Janet's car was out of sight. Then, closing the door, she glanced up the stairs and said, "Well, we certainly put her in her place, didn't we, Winifred?"

But she would not have felt so sure of that if she could have got into Janet's mind as she drove away.

There was something funny going on about Winifred, the

latter was thinking. The way Rita had acted upstairs, for instance, making such a big deal of not even letting her get a look inside the closet.

Also, except for the two pictures and a few odds and ends around, the room didn't seem personal enough in the way that most rooms did. No matter how neat she kept it Winifred should have more pictures, more things of hers around. As for the pictures she had on display, that one of her parents on their wedding day was ridiculous, not at all the style anyone would expect from a woman like her.

There was the bathroom too. Not a thing in the medicine chest that seemed to belong to her. Janet had looked—she always looked in people's medicine chests—and could recall nothing added to what had been there when Rita lived alone.

There was the point, of course, that Winifred, going away for the weekend, had taken her toothbrush, toothpaste, and make-up with her—all of it, though, for just a couple of days? It seemed as if a woman with her well-groomed appearance would have a whole assortment of make-up to choose from as well as a fully equipped cosmetic case for traveling. Janet had one herself—with an extra toothbrush and toothpaste in it—and always took it on trips so as not to have to hunt around for things.

Did Winifred have just one set of cosmetics and have to strip her bureau of them whenever she went anywhere?

Not necessarily, Janet decided after a moment's thought. She might keep lots more in one of her bureau drawers. There'd been no chance to open them with Rita hovering every minute. She had acted as if she expected Janet to steal something belonging to her precious Winifred.

Why had she acted that way? Not only upstairs in Winifred's room but before that too. Her manner had been snippy from the start. She hadn't even offered a drink until Janet asked for one herself. It wasn't a bit like her to be so inhospitable. It was more poor old Rita's thing to overdo the hospitality bit.

Did Ted come into it? Of course not. There was no way she could have found out he had dropped her for Janet.

Which meant that all the funny business tonight was connected with Winifred.

How long had Rita known her? She wouldn't say that day at lunch. Wouldn't say much of anything, in fact, except that her new roommate's name was Winifred Lawton, that she was divorced and worked as a cocktail hostess at The Blue Grotto.

Now that she had seen Winifred's picture Janet felt more at sea than ever over their friendship. Winifred didn't seem to be Rita's type at all. Or rather, Rita didn't seem to be Winifred's.

Why would anyone like her take up with Rita? Or, even more to the point, want to get stuck with her in her little house on a country road, practically in the back of beyond?

There was certainly something very peculiar about it; something being covered up . . .

The more Janet thought about it, the less prepared she was to let it drop. She not only had more than her share of curiosity, she particularly disliked the feeling of not being in the center of whatever was going on, of having things hidden from her.

Which meant, she told herself as she neared home, that she wasn't going to let Rita get away with all this mystery about Winifred. If she thought for one minute that she could be so snippy to Janet and keep everything connected with Winifred to herself, she had another think coming.

But considering the way she had acted tonight, Janet couldn't just drop in on her again very soon in the hope of meeting her roommate.

Then what should her next move be?

She thought suddenly of Mrs. Wheelock who lived right across the street from Sally Glenn, a nurse she was friendly with. She had recognized the building on her first visit at Sally's. She hadn't seen the older woman that day or on any of her later visits, not at all, in fact, since their chance meeting at 7 Corners.

Still, no reason why she shouldn't stop by this coming Sunday.

Janet thought it over. The occasion, a brunch at Sally's, fitted in perfectly. Visit Mrs. Wheelock first, try to pump her about Winifred. She could at least find out if Mrs. Wheelock had met her yet and, if she had, what her impression of her was.

The more Janet thought about it, the better she liked the idea. She began to rehearse her opening speech. "Hi, Mrs. Wheelock, how are you? I'm on my way to visit a friend across the street, and it dawned on me as I got out of my car that this was where you lived. So I thought I'd drop in for a few minutes."

It struck just the right casual note. It should produce some information about Winifred. And when it got back to Rita it would serve notice on her not to be so snippy the next time.

XIII

Sunday afternoon, with Janet's visit on her mind, Mrs. Wheelock tried to call Rita but she had been invited out to dinner and there was no answer.

Mrs. Wheelock let it go until she arrived at the office Monday morning and had responded to all the greetings and questions about her trip. Then, when Rita and she were by themselves, she said, "Janet dropped by to see me yesterday right after I got home from the airport."

"Oh?" Rita made it a question, although she knew what was to come next.

"She was looking for information about Winifred. Really Rita," Mrs. Wheelock's laugh had an exasperated edge, "now that she's moved in with you, I hope there'll be no more surprises over her. Yesterday was the second time I was completely at sea when Janet brought her up. She moved in, I gather, while I was gone?"

"Yes. Janet came Friday night to return my coffee pot and asked all kinds of questions about her. Winifred wasn't there. She was away for the weekend."

"So Janet informed me," Mrs. Wheelock said dryly. "She seemed frustrated not to have had a chance to meet her."

"What a pest she is," Rita said pouring their morning coffee, considering what she should do about Winifred now that there was this new development. The best thing, she decided, was to let a couple of weeks go by and then say that Winifred had left, given up her job and gone back to New York State. It wasn't as if Mrs. Wheelock came to Rita's house all that often. Sometimes it was a month, perhaps, between visits.

It was a relief to tell herself this; to realize that there was still plenty of time before she had to let go of Winifred.

Less reassuring, however, was Rita's realization that she felt a sense of loss at the prospect of letting go of her at all.

That wasn't good; that was carrying her involvement with Winifred past the point of a silly little game that could be cut off at a moment's notice.

She put that thought away from her as she drank her coffee.

At lunch that day she asked Mrs. Wheelock, "What did Janet have to say?"

"Oh, she hinted around trying to find out if I knew when and where you met Winifred and then she wanted to know if I'd met her yet myself. She got very little out of me and went away, I imagine, twice as frustrated as when she arrived. How's it going so far having Winifred with you?"

"Perfectly fine," Rita said and then, thinking of future contingencies, "not that I've seen much of her up until now. She has all these mixed-up hours, you see, like going in one day at eleven and not until five the next."

"Really? I don't know a thing about that sort of job but I suppose a place that starts with lunch and goes on through dinner until late at night would have to be run like that."

"Oh yes," said Rita who knew nothing about it herself but felt that she had gained an even lengthier reprieve through mentioning it. Weeks and weeks could go by and no matter whether Mrs. Wheelock came to see her in the daytime or at night she could say Winifred was working. Mrs. Wheelock wasn't nosy like Janet. If she used the bathroom, she wouldn't dream of going into Winifred's room.

Rita corrected the thought. Winifred's room—if Winifred existed.

But there was still Janet to deal with. Having got nowhere with Mrs. Wheelock, she wouldn't let the matter rest there.

Janet! She had fastened herself onto Rita's life, using and

disrupting it ever since the ill-omened day Rita had invited her to dinner.

A succubus, that was Janet.

What was she going to do about her? There must be something she could do, some way to get rid of her once and for all . . .

At the end of that week Rita was faced with another example of Janet's persistence. It took the form of a phone call Friday night after dinner while Rita was working in her garden, enjoying the mild spring evening, not even thinking about Winifred or about Janet herself.

She would have let the phone ring unanswered if she had known who was calling but as it was, she hurried in through the back door, gave her dirt-caked hands a quick rinse at the sink and picked up the phone next to it.

"Hi, Rita, it's me," Janet said brightly.

"Yes?" Rita's tone was distant.

"I was beginning to think you weren't home."

"I'm working in the yard. I bought some plants today that I want to put in before dark so unless it's something special—"

"Well, not really—except that I was wondering if you'd be free some night next week to come over and have a drink at my place." Janet paused. "You and Winifred. I'm looking forward to meeting her."

So there it was. Rita was so enraged that she didn't trust herself to speak.

"I'll be free either Tuesday or Friday night whichever suits you best," Janet continued.

Rita took a deep breath and regained self-control. "I'm afraid neither one would work out," she said. "I already have plans for Friday night and I know Winifred isn't free Tuesday. She happened to mention at breakfast this morning that she's going out to dinner Tuesday night."

"Oh." Janet was silent in thought and then said on a reluctant note, "Well, I guess we'll have to postpone it until the following week."

"I'm not sure about that week either," Rita replied. "I already have a couple of things in mind for it myself and I certainly can't speak for Winifred considering how often her work schedule changes. Some days she goes in early to cover lunch; other days she doesn't go in until the cocktail hour and is there until the place closes at one o'clock. Or she might work a broken shift; three or four hours off in the afternoon and then go back for the dinner crowd."

Details of Winifred's work schedule tripped off Rita's tongue. Regardless of its accuracy, it sounded plausible enough to her and apparently to Janet who did not question it.

Instead, she went off on a new tack that caught Rita unawares, asking, "Did you meet Winifred at The Blue Grotto?"

"No." But that answer couldn't stand alone. "Through a friend in Washington." Rita hesitated but not knowing what the future held where Winifred was concerned added prudently, "Just a few months ago. Last fall, in fact."

"Oh." Janet kept satisfaction out of her voice that at least she had extracted the information that it wasn't a friendship of long standing. Then she said, "Talk to Winifred, anyway, about coming over. Perhaps we'll be able to work out something for the week after next. Give me a ring when you find out what nights she'll be free."

"I may not be free the same night myself."

"Let me know anyway."

"Yes." Rita said good-by and hung up without thanking Janet for the invitation.

Rage seized her again on her way outdoors. She sought an outlet for it by trying to slam the screen door after her but the governor would only let it close gently.

This was one of the moments, she thought, assaulting the ground with her trowel, when the hatred she felt toward Janet almost scared her.

Mostly over Ted, yes, but Janet herself with her pushiness certainly added to the violence of Rita's feeling.

It was getting dark by the time she finished her planting and put her gardening tools away in the garage. She had worked off her turbulent mood and took quiet pleasure in what she had accomplished that night.

All she had on her mind as she headed for the back door was a shower followed by a nightcap while she read the evening paper.

But then her eye fell on a clump of daffodils in full bloom. She would cut a few of them and a few grape hyacinths too and take them in the house.

She arranged them in a pretty old vase, started to set it on a table in the living room but instead took it upstairs and put it on the desk in Winifred's room.

More and more often lately she had begun to think of it that way without the qualifying thought—if Winifred existed—coming into her mind.

When she had taken a shower and was ready to go downstairs she glanced into Winifred's room—there was that thought again—to admire the flowers. They looked lovely; they always dressed up a room.

But then her eyes went to the flowered curtains. Weren't they a little dingy? The clear true colors of the fresh flowers really showed them up. She had better drop them off at the cleaner's Monday on her way to work.

While she was making herself a drink her thoughts reverted to Janet. The only way to handle her was to ignore her completely. Sooner or later, no matter how thick-skinned she was, it would dawn on her that Rita had no intention of accepting any invitation of hers, to say nothing of letting her meet Winifred.

But with Mrs. Wheelock the situation was entirely different.

She had invited Rita to dinner that Sunday. The day was still so warm and bright when Rita arrived at five o'clock that she served drinks on her balcony.

They were having refills before Rita brought up the phone call from Janet Friday night.

Mrs. Wheelock shook her head over it. "She really is making a nuisance of herself. Have you mentioned it to Winifred?"

"No. I don't intend to either."

The older woman gave it thought, settling her trim figure

deeper in her basket chair. "Blatant," she commented. "You never heard a word from her for weeks after that Saturday—"

"When she took Ted away from me, you mean? Except for the day I met her at 7 Corners, I never expected to hear from her again."

"Her guilty conscience."

"I doubt she's got any kind of conscience at all," Rita said on a hard note. "But now she's got this hang-up on Winifred. She's fascinated by her job—thinks it's glamorous, I guess—and by her looks too since she saw the snapshot of her in her room."

"Oh, she has one on display? What does she look like? All you've ever said was how attractive she was."

Rita stirred restively but reminded herself that it was she who had brought Winifred into the conversation, a disturbing element in this peaceful hour on the balcony.

"Oh, is that all I've told you?" she said. "Well, Winifred has lovely auburn hair and blue eyes. She's slim and elegant-looking and dresses elegantly too. She's like a model in a fashion magazine."

"That sounds intriguing," Mrs. Wheelock said looking at Rita with the thought that while she was attractive enough she was too big ever to be called elegant herself. Then, just as Janet had, she wondered what had led a woman like Winifred with a job like hers to move in with Rita out in the country instead of taking an apartment in Washington more convenient to where she worked, more in the center of things.

But Mrs. Wheelock, thinking of them as only chance acquaintances, had even more to wonder about than Janet who regarded them as friends and had no idea that all Rita really knew about Winifred was whatever the latter chose to tell her.

That was the point that concerned Mrs. Wheelock the most; her realization that Rita, lonely as she was, and still naive in many ways, would be all too ready to gloss over any gaps in Winifred's recital.

Now there was this added bit about her looks and style.

What could have led her, Mrs. Wheelock asked herself again, to take up with Rita?

From all indications, she seemed worldly enough to have recognized the traits in Rita that created difficulties when it came to sharing her home with anyone. And yet she had elected to go ahead with it.

It was more than just a little peculiar. It was almost—well, worrisome.

The subject was dropped. After dinner, though, having coffee in the living room, Mrs. Wheelock brought it up again. "I don't want to seem like Janet, Rita, but I must say I'd like to meet Winifred myself."

Rita's heart sank. "Why, yes, of course. I want you to. We'll have to arrange it."

"You might bring her over for a drink or something. Oh dear," Mrs. Wheelock laughed ruefully. "Now I do sound exactly like Janet."

"No indeed," Rita protested. "After all, we're friends and it's only natural you'd want to meet Winifred. With Janet it's just plain nosiness."

"Well I'm thankful you don't lump us together!"

"I don't know just when we can work it out, though," Rita continued on a cautious note. "Winifred's so busy she's hardly home at all and then, as I told you, her work schedule changes so much."

"No hurry," said Mrs. Wheelock catching the cautious note. Rita, she thought, saw very little of Winifred Lawton and could make no demands on her time. Was even, perhaps, a little out of her depth with her.

In fact, looking back over the past week since her return from her vacation, Mrs. Wheelock realized that Rita hadn't said much about her new roommate, whereas Louise Brooks and her predecessors had figured largely in her conversation. In other words, Winifred seemed to be keeping her at a distance.

Mrs. Wheelock found that reassuring. It indicated that Winifred considered her association with Rita as a business matter of two people living under the same roof and sharing expenses. It was certainly going to cost her far less than maintaining her own apartment.

Was money the answer to why she was there? How much did she earn at The Blue Grotto?

Mrs. Wheelock hadn't the least idea. It crossed her mind, though, that if she was right about Winifred's attitude, it might lead to a better understanding than Rita had been able to establish with previous roommates from whom she had expected a closer relationship than they were prepared to offer.

Viewed in that light, Winifred seemed even more interesting. Mrs. Wheelock looked forward to meeting her.

XIV

It was just too stupid, feeling so depressed all of a sudden, Rita told herself driving home from Mrs. Wheelock's that night. Hadn't she known from the start that Winifred was no more than a silly game, a passing fancy to tide her over an unhappy interlude in her life? She had been lucky, really, to get away with it as long as this. She wouldn't have been able to get away with it at all except that she had never mentioned Winifred to anyone aside from Mrs. Wheelock and Janet. If it hadn't been for Janet, the way she kept needling Rita that day at lunch, the whole concept of Winifred would never have entered Rita's mind.

But since then Winifred had somehow, little by little, taken on a personality of her own with the looks and style and job that seemed just right for her.

That was all nonsense, though. No, not all of it, considering things that had happened in the past and the odd moments of comfort Winifred brought Rita in the present.

Now, however, much sooner than she was ready to, she would have to let Winifred go. Mrs. Wheelock had brought that home tonight by saying that she, too, would like to meet her. Even though her attitude was poles apart from Janet's, it still meant the end of Winifred.

Janet's prying could be coped with; but Mrs. Wheelock's perfectly natural interest in Rita's new roommate was a different matter.

Excuses would soon wear thin. The only real solution to not producing Winifred was to let her go.

Rita tried to shake off the weight of that prospect as her house came into view, resorting to the familiar litany, "There is no Winifred; she doesn't exist." Turning in at her driveway she enlarged upon it. "All those things upstairs that are supposed to be hers are just odds and ends from junk boxes. Her room isn't really her room because she doesn't exist and never will exist outside my head."

But reciting such down-to-earth truths only deepened Rita's sense of desolation.

The house had a dark and empty look walking over to it from the garage. She had intended to turn on the back light before she left that afternoon but had forgotten to as she often did when leaving in broad daylight. She should turn on a light inside as well as out, she thought, fumbling with the door key in the dark. An inside light was supposed to be a safeguard against burglars. Preferably an upstairs light, the articles written about it said.

The next thought that crossed her mind was that a light left on upstairs in Winifred's room would be a welcoming note coming home.

Once again, unlocking the door, she reminded herself that Winifred didn't exist.

But going upstairs to bed her footsteps turned of their own accord into Winifred's room.

It looked bare without the curtains, already taken down to go to the cleaner's tomorrow. They would look much better, though, when they came back.

It was too bad she hadn't had them cleaned weeks ago. Now there was only a short time left before she had to let Winifred go.

But why couldn't she still pretend after that, here by herself, that this was still Winifred's room?

No, it wouldn't be at all the same. Being able to talk about her to Mrs. Wheelock—even Janet—gave her substance.

Well, at least it didn't have to be right away. Things could go on as they were for another two or three weeks.

That thought offered little comfort to Rita as she went to bed.

She lay long awake. Sleep, when it came, was troubled by a series of dreams that had no connection except for an underlying theme of fear and stress. In one of them, the only one she could reconstruct in detail the next morning, she was back in Granville walking along Main Street wearing the green dress Dolly had worn that last day of her life and teetering on high heels as she had teetered. In the dream Rita tried to hurry aware of something threatening her if she didn't get home right away but somehow caught up in incidents that held her back: a policeman who wanted to know where she was going; a street barricade outside a bank; a crowd at a corner that wouldn't let her pass; a rambling tour of the department store where her mother had bought the green dress but where no one would speak to her as she ran from section to section in desperate search of another dress like it.

That dream faded into others. In one of them, Winifred stood in the middle of her room wearing the green dress, furious over where the rest of her clothes were. Rita scurried about frantically but couldn't find them. Winifred raised her hand with some sort of weapon in it and screamed at her to get out of her room. Rita fled downstairs and out onto the patio where Ted Parker and Janet sat hand in hand laughing at her.

She awoke at first light trembling from some final bad dream that vanished before she opened her eyes.

The hands on her bedside clock said quarter of six. She tried to go back to sleep but sleep escaped her in spite of her restless night.

She got up sluggishly a little after six o'clock. A shower would help, she thought, heading for the bathroom. She glanced into Winifred's room on the way and stopped short, sluggishness shocked out of her.

The room was in chaos, drawers hanging open, everything on top of the bureau in an upside-down clutter, scatter rugs kicked up, bed torn apart, vase of flowers knocked over, curtains left neatly folded on the rush-bottomed chair yesterday now a tangled heap on the floor beside the desk.

"Winifred?" Rita's voice, sharp with fright, shattered the early morning quiet and brought her back to reality.

She had created this chaos herself. In her sleep.

But why? Reality was almost as frightening as her first superstitious reaction had been. Until last night she hadn't sleepwalked since her childhood.

All these years later, what had brought it on?

Well, lack of sleep, for one thing; and bad dreams that broke up what little she'd had. They were enough to make anyone sleepwalk.

Or were they?

Yes. No need to look for a more complicated answer; the simplest one was usually the right one.

Rita tidied up the room, made the bed, folded the curtains and put them by the door to take downstairs with her.

It was a relief to get the room back in order with nothing to show that sometime during the night she had reverted to the sleepwalking of her childhood.

Except that it was not quite the same for in that earlier time she had displayed none of the violence that had taken possession of her last night.

Had it sprung from some sort of deep-buried hostility toward Winifred?

She thrust the unbidden question away from her. It was too ridiculous. How could she feel hostility toward someone who didn't exist?

She took a shower and got dressed. Combing her hair in front of her mirror she couldn't miss seeing the toll taken by the night; the shadowed drawn look on her face, the grayness under the olive tones of her complexion that almost seemed to match the pale gray of her eyes.

She turned away from the mirror quickly and went downstairs.

The kitchen was bright with sunshine. The window by the

table looked out on the garden with its colorful array of bulbs in bloom. But Rita's mood could not be lightened by the spring morning. It could not remove from her the residue of fear last night had left behind.

It stayed with her on her way to work, the curtains on the car seat beside her. She looked at them now and then out of the corner of her eye. Winifred's curtains . . .

During the morning her thoughts kept returning to last night. Her need to talk to Mrs. Wheelock about it grew until at last a way to bring it up, an edited version of it, occurred to her.

Over lunch would be the best time.

She waited until they were served at the coffee shop they went to and then began, "Last night turned out to be quite some night after I got home from your place, Mrs. Wheelock."

"What happened?"

"First of all, I had a hard time getting to sleep—one of those nights, y'know?—and when I finally did I kept having these horrible mixed-up dreams."

"Nightmares, you mean?"

"Not really. Sort of scary, though, and weird. The worst one was about Winifred. She was standing in the middle of her room demanding to know what I had done with her clothes. When I couldn't find them she started screaming at me to get out. She had a weapon of some kind in her hand—I couldn't quite see what it was—but in the dream I knew she was threatening me with it and I ran downstairs—" Rita paused but felt impelled to tell the rest of it.

"I ran out the back door," she said on a falling note, "and there on my patio were Janet and Ted holding hands and laughing at me."

"You certainly did have a bad night."

"That wasn't the half of it. Winifred sleepwalked."

"Oh no."

"Oh yes. I couldn't imagine what was going on when all this banging and thumping woke me up. It scared me stiff until I realized it was coming from Winifred's room and that her door was open and her light shining under my door. I got up and went into her room and oh, Mrs. Wheelock, you should have seen it!"

"What was the matter with it?"

"She had torn everything apart; her bed, her bureau, the curtains I'd taken down to go to the cleaner's, the rugs, everything. Just as I walked in, she knocked over a vase of flowers on the desk. I said, 'Winifred, what are you doing?' and my voice was so sharp that it woke her up. She was in a complete daze at first. After a minute or two she began to cry about the way I'd frightened her."

"Seems to me that I've read you're not supposed to wake people up too suddenly when they're sleepwalking," Mrs. Wheelock commented. "Not that I've ever known anyone who did."

"I used to myself for a while after—well, when I was a kid. I don't remember how my parents handled it. Anyway, I didn't know Winifred was sleepwalking when I woke her up."

"What time was all this?"

"Just coming daylight. I had her sit down while I made up her bed and got her room straightened out. She cried the whole time. It was quite an experience."

"I'm sure it was. What did she say when she calmed down?"

"Nothing much really. She got back into bed and asked me to close her door on my way out."

Mrs. Wheelock raised her eyebrows. "That was all? Was she still more or less in a daze?"

"Perhaps."

"Did you see her before you left for work?"

"Yes, just before. She came downstairs in her robe and poured herself a cup of coffee. She was very quiet and didn't say a word about her sleepwalking."

"Not a word?" Mrs. Wheelock shook her head. "How could she act that way? She should have said something about what brought it on and apologized for the upset it caused you. But with her attitude, I don't think I'd feel very comfortable myself living in the same house with her."

"Yes, it was rather odd," Rita said neutrally. It hadn't occurred to her at the start of her much revised account of last night's events that not only would she find an outlet in Mrs. Wheelock for discussing them but would also be giving herself grounds for letting go of Winifred.

She still needn't be in too great a hurry about it, though.

"I hope it won't happen again," Mrs. Wheelock said presently.

"So do I." Rita tried to sound casual, a step removed from it all, but the older woman didn't miss the hesitant note in her voice.

"I'm afraid you're going to feel nervous now, living in the same house with Winifred," she said. "Anyone would. It's not as if you'd known her a long time. She's still practically a stranger to you. And as it's turned out, a sleepwalking stranger."

"No, not a stranger. I told you how congenial I found her from the first time we met."

"Well, you certainly can't call her an old friend on such short acquaintance."

Rita had no answer to that. Winifred wasn't mentioned again during the rest of lunch or on the way back to the office. But when they arrived Mrs. Wheelock asked, "Wouldn't you rather go back to living alone after last night?"

Here was another opportunity for letting go of Winifred but once again Rita couldn't bring herself to take advantage of it.

"Oh, I don't know," she said. "I'll have to wait and see."

Just a little while longer, she thought. Just another week or so. Then she would put an end to it.

XV

Rita went to bed that night and for a night or two thereafter apprehensive of another sleepwalking incident. By Thursday, when there hadn't been one, the new image of Winifred as a potentially hostile rather than companionable figure began to fade out of her mind.

When Mrs. Wheelock asked if she had mentioned her sleepwalking yet, Rita replied in a tone that did not invite discussion of it, "No, she hasn't said a word about it and neither have I. It's just as well, I guess."

Thursday night she hung the curtains, back from the cleaner's, in Winifred's room and cut flowers for it. As she put them on the desk her glance fell on the blotter. Shouldn't it look more used? No, it didn't really matter. Ball-point pens didn't leave ink blots.

The curtains looked so fresh and crisp that the bedspread now seemed a little dingy by comparison. Rita whisked it downstairs, ran it through the washer and dryer and had it back on the bed the moment it was dry. Then she decided to polish the furniture.

It shone by the time she was finished. She puttered around, straightening the paper knife on the desk, smoothing the folds of the curtains.

As she gave the room a final inspection the ambivalent feelings she'd had toward it since her sleepwalking Sunday night vanished completely. She had been letting her imagination run away with her over it, conjuring up a hostile atmosphere—

almost a hostile presence—in the room, working herself up into being a little uneasy about going into it.

But now it was once again the pretty friendly room it had been before Sunday night.

The next few days were uneventful. Except for going to a party Saturday night Rita devoted most of her free time to her garden.

Janet Murray was farthest from her mind when she called the following Tuesday evening.

"Hi, Rita, it's me again," she began on her usual chatty note.

"Yes," said Rita. "How are you?"

"Well, terribly busy. That's why I thought I'd better call. I've been out so much this past week that I wondered if you'd tried to reach me and hadn't been able to."

"No, I haven't called you at all."

"Really? Last time we talked, wasn't it left that you'd check with Winifred to find out when she'd be free this week so that we could all get together?"

What was the matter with Janet, hanging on like this, refusing to take no for an answer?

Well, all Rita could do was try again. "I'm afraid it won't work out any better this week than last," she said. "So why not just let it go for a while?" After a pause she added, "It's really not important enough to push, Janet, having us drop in for a drink."

"I guess not. But I do want to meet Winifred."

"I know you do. You've made it very clear. On the other hand, I don't feel I should make a big deal out of it with her."

"No, that wouldn't do. Still, there must be some evenings when you're both home and I am too. Like tonight, for instance. I'm not doing anything if you don't mind the short notice."

"But Winifred's gone out." It took effort for Rita to keep her tone matter-of-fact. "She has a dinner date tonight. That's the way it is most nights she isn't working. It's hard to pin her down to anything."

"Oh." Janet evoked a picture of the glamorous Winifred having dinner with a handsome man who took her to some very special restaurant as expensive as The Blue Grotto itself. She felt a pang of envy. The most she could hope for herself tonight was that Sam Richards would call her when he got off duty and ask her out for a hamburger.

She soothed her envy with a small gibe. "Doesn't seem as if Winifred's much company for you."

"We get along fine. Even double-date occasionally."

"Do you? How nice. Well, I'd better hang up now. I'll be in touch."

No doubt about that, Rita thought sourly as she hung up herself. Spoiled rotten, used to getting her own way, that was Janet. Once she made up her mind to something, she just wouldn't let go.

Right now she had made up her mind that she wanted to meet Winifred and the more Rita stalled her off, the more persistent she became.

Was she going to keep it up until she forced Rita to say Winifred was no longer with her? Hadn't she already done her enough harm without that?

It seemed not. It seemed that there was no way to get rid of her.

"God, how I loathe her!" Rita's voice shook with anger. "What am I going to do if she doesn't let me alone?"

The answer to that question was all too plain. She would have to say Winifred had moved back to New York State.

Well, she had to say that very soon anyway, didn't she, for Mrs. Wheelock's benefit?

Yes, but she still wanted to be able to decide for herself just when she would do it, not have the decision forced on her by Janet.

She went outside. She had planned to prune the forsythia tonight and there was no point in allowing Janet to upset her schedule on that too.

Rita got her clippers from the garage and set to work. And once again, as after that other infuriating call from Janet, she found an outlet for her feelings in bringing the same savage intensity to her task.

And like that other time, it had the same calming effect on her by the time it was finished.

She made herself a drink and sat down on the patio with it in the twilight. Might as well face it, she reflected, sipping from her glass. She had to start paving the way for letting go of Winifred.

How soon?

Well, not tomorrow. She needn't be in that great a rush. Next week, perhaps. That was soon enough.

She thought she had resigned herself to it when she went to bed. But that didn't prevent her from already feeling a sense of loss as she halted in the doorway to Winifred's room and said softly, "Good night, Winifred."

That night she dreamed about her again. The dream began in a vague shadowy way with her surroundings not at all clear. Then she realized that she was on her way out of her own room. It was in darkness but light shone into it from Winifred's room across the hall where the door stood open.

There was no sign of Winifred. She didn't answer when Rita spoke to her. Even so, there was nothing out of the ordinary, nothing frightening about the scene at first. But as Rita started to go downstairs she suddenly became aware of Winifred close behind her, the dark silk dress she wore in the picture rustling at every step. When Rita moved faster Winifred quickened her pace too.

At the foot of the stairs the dream turned into a nightmare with Rita running through the living room not looking back, terrified of what she would see. She ran out into the kitchen and over to the table backing up against it, opening the drawer with one hand and groping inside it.

When she looked up Winifred stood in the doorway in the dark silk dress. But above it instead of the faintly smiling face in the picture was a grinning skull, a child's skull, much too small for the body of a woman.

"Dolly!" she screamed and woke herself up screaming.

She looked about her confusedly not quite knowing for a few moments where she was. As the first shock of the dream passed she saw that she was in her kitchen; alone in it with no skull-topped figure in the doorway.

The overhead light was on. She was standing by the table with a knife in her hand and blood oozing from a cut on her thumb.

She walked slowly over to the sink and washed the blood off. The cut was small and shallow. A Band-Aid would take care of it.

The room felt chilly. She shook with cold in her thin night-gown.

What time was it? The clock said half-past four.

She had sleepwalked again.

She went back upstairs turning off the kitchen light on the way. But she was not left in darkness. Light from upstairs shone in the front hall. From Winifred's room. When she had got out of bed during the dream—the nightmare—she had turned that light on too.

She didn't look in the room as she went past it to get a Band-Aid in the bathroom.

Her cut had already stopped bleeding. It didn't amount to anything. But its implications did.

She still avoided looking in the other room when she turned off the light. She didn't want to think about going in there walking in her sleep to turn it on before she went downstairs with Winifred's rustling step behind her.

There was no Winifred. She didn't exist. And Dolly was long years in her grave.

Rita went back to bed and put her electric blanket on high heat until its warmth took away the icy coldness that shook her whole body.

She didn't try to go back to sleep. Already light touched her windows facing south and east. Propped up on pillows she watched it strengthen, the first deep red rays on the horizon spread and soften into the clear pink of sunrise. It flooded her room, leaving no shadows to foster the kind of fears that came in the dark.

Did they still linger in Winifred's room?

The way to find out was to confront them.

Rita got out of bed, went purposefully across the hall and then hesitated in the doorway. With windows looking north and west, untouched by the sunrise, the room did not look welcoming in the gray light. But she had experienced that same feeling of an unfriendly atmosphere in it when she had sleepwalked before, she reminded herself. It was only natural, part of the aftermath to it. There was nothing at all to be afraid of in the room itself.

She went over to the bureau, got the snapshot out of the mirror frame and took it back to her room to look at it in the brighter light.

It looked the same, the faintly smiling face of the unknown woman. She had studied it so often, always with pleasure, that she knew it by heart.

What change had she expected—that the woman had grown horns in the night? No, hardly that, but still—

My God, am I going nuts or something? Rita asked herself. I'd better get out of this house for a while.

She flung herself into jeans and a sweater, thrust her feet into loafers and went out into the yard.

But not to work. She sat down on the patio and let the freshness of the early May morning wash over her, listening to the chorus of birds.

Not always a musical chorus, she reflected presently, finding diversion in the piercing cries of a red-winged blackbird driving other birds away from the feeder and then by a raucous quarrel two bluejays carried on. Birds, in or out of their nests, did not agree.

She felt much more relaxed when she went back into the house to fix breakfast and get ready for work.

But when she went upstairs she found herself looking through a snapshot album for pictures of Dolly. She picked out one that was Dolly to the life standing on the front steps laughing with her head tipped back.

Rita took it into Winifred's room and put it in the mirror frame above the picture of the unknown woman.

"Your niece, Winifred," she told the woman. "Or would you rather it was goddaughter?"

It didn't matter. Either way the picture seemed right. Dolly, innocent laughing child, would ward off bad dreams.

But to be on the safe side, Rita took a further step. She got out a bunch of old keys and found one that fitted the lock on her bedroom door. She would lock herself in at night until she got over her spell of sleepwalking.

She would not listen to the inner voice that said she should tell Mrs. Wheelock today that Winifred was leaving.

XVI

Mrs. Wheelock noticed the Band-Aid on Rita's thumb soon after she arrived at the office.

"How'd you do that?" she asked.

"The knife slipped. It's just a small cut."

This time Rita did not want to talk about her sleepwalking. That would bring it all back. Not talking about it would help make it go away.

It was bowling night. Afterward she invited the members of her bowling team back to the house for a drink. It was better than going home alone worrying about what kind of a night she would have.

The group stayed until almost eleven-thirty. Rita took the precaution of locking herself into her room when she went to bed but otherwise tried not to think about anything connected with Winifred. She slept soundly through the night and continued to do so for the rest of the week.

She invited Mrs. Wheelock to dinner that Sunday. "There'll be just the two of us," she said. "Winifred's going away for the weekend."

"Oh, is she going home for Mother's Day?"

"No, she's visiting some friend in Philadelphia. I'm sorry you won't get to meet her. It never seems to work out so that you do."

"Well, it will have advantages Sunday too," Mrs. Wheelock said. "We can talk about anything we like without her there.

Even though, from what you've told me, she's easy to get acquainted with."

"Sometimes." Rita hesitated and then couldn't stop herself from adding, "Other times she doesn't seem as—well, as friendly as she did at first."

It had a familiar sound to Mrs. Wheelock—Rita beginning to find fault with a roommate—but she made no comment.

Sunday turned out to be a perfect day. As they sat outside on the patio Rita looked around her sunlit yard and said, "There can't be any place in the world more beautiful than Virginia at this time of year."

"It would be hard to find," Mrs. Wheelock agreed. "Your iris is just lovely, all the different colors."

Their conversation went on like that with comfortable silences falling now and then.

Rita served dinner outdoors. While she was getting ready to bring it out Mrs. Wheelock went upstairs to the bathroom. On her way down she paused to glance into Winifred's room and thought that from the way she kept it she must be as neat as Rita herself. That was certainly in her favor after Louise Brooks's untidiness. Even the desk, where people tended to allow themselves some leeway, was in perfect order. There was a brilliant display of iris on it that looked too fresh for Winifred to have cut them before she left Friday.

"Dinner's ready." Rita came to the foot of the stairs. When she saw Mrs. Wheelock in the doorway to Winifred's room, she said anxiously, "Oh dear, you haven't touched anything in there, have you? Winifred's terribly fussy about her things."

"Now, Rita, you know better than that," Mrs. Wheelock chided her. "I was just looking in, noticing how neat it is and admiring the iris. They look so fresh you must have cut them for her today."

"Yes. She loves flowers. I thought they'd be a nice surprise for her when she gets home late tonight."

"She should be pleased." Mrs. Wheelock came downstairs.

"I'll cut you some before you leave."

"I really wasn't hinting," Mrs. Wheelock said with a rueful

smile. "I already have the beautiful flowers Keith sent me for Mother's Day."

"I know. Now you'll have some more."

After dinner Rita cut the iris for Mrs. Wheelock to take home with her.

The warmth of the day lingered. They stayed outdoors while the sunset flamed across the sky and the long May twilight set in.

"What a marvelous day it's been," Mrs. Wheelock said as Rita poured cordials for them. "I must say, though, that I don't envy Winifred her drive back from Philadelphia tonight. She'll have plenty of traffic to cope with. What kind of a car does she have?"

"Car?" Rita's mind went blank for a moment. "Oh, a Pinto."

Another comfortable silence fell while they sipped their cordials. Then, suddenly, without any intention of bringing it up, without even realizing it was on her mind, Rita blurted out, "Winifred sleepwalked again the other night."

"Oh no."

"Yes, she did."

"Was it as bad as the first time?"

"Well, she didn't tear her room apart again, but in another way it was worse."

"How?"

"She had a knife in her hand when I woke up—" Rita broke off, disconcerted by her slip of the tongue and then hurried on, "I mean, when I went downstairs after I woke up—she must have done something that woke me—and there she was in the kitchen with the light on holding the knife."

"Good heavens," Mrs. Wheelock said in a shocked voice.

"That's how I cut my thumb, taking it away from her." Rita's glance rested on the thin red line of the nearly healed cut. But what she actually saw, quite vividly, was Winifred standing by the table where she had stood herself with the same hostile look on her face that she'd had in the earlier dream. It seemed so real for a moment that Rita could almost see herself going over to Winifred, talking in a soothing voice while she took the knife away from her and through nervousness cut her own thumb in the process.

If she carried the imagery even farther, right about now Winifred was setting out on her trip home from Philadelphia. . . .

Rita gave herself a mental shake that brought her back to reality. Winifred did not exist.

Why had she told the story at all, weaving truth and lies together? It didn't change the situation to bring her concern over her sleepwalking out into the open. Even if she had been able to talk about it with complete honesty, Mrs. Wheelock had no magic wand that would put an end to it. Somehow, she had to work it out herself.

"Did you wake her up after you took the knife away from her?" Mrs. Wheelock asked.

"She woke up herself and was terribly upset when she realized she had sleepwalked again."

"I should think so." Mrs. Wheelock set her cordial glass down. "Was she ready to talk about it this time?"

"Yes. We sat and talked until the sun came up. She went through a spell of sleepwalking in her childhood just as I did but she said it hadn't happened since."

"How recently was she divorced?"

Rita seized on the question. It offered, in a sense, some parallel to her own uncertainties of the past few months. "Very recently. Right before she came to Washington and started working at The Blue Grotto."

"And not long after that moved in with you," Mrs. Wheelock said musingly. "There's been a lot of change in her life on top of her divorce. It must be a time of stress for her."

A time of stress, thought Rita. That was what she was going through; it explained her nightmares, her sleepwalking. Even though they centered on Winifred, that was a side issue, not the heart of Rita's problem.

"But still, there's no getting around the knife," Mrs. Wheelock continued. "Did she tell you how it fitted into whatever nightmare brought on her sleepwalking?"

"She said it had nothing to do with it. The dream didn't even frighten her at first, she said, but then going downstairs she heard footsteps right behind her."

In the twilight Rita's shiver at the memory of it went unnoticed by Mrs. Wheelock who said, "I've had that dream of being followed myself. It's a horrid one."

"She didn't dare turn around when she got to the foot of the stairs, not wanting to see who it was. She ran out into the kitchen." Rita paused to expurgate. "The next thing she knew I had just taken the knife from her."

"Sounds as if it was to defend herself against whoever—or whatever—was behind her in the dream," said Mrs. Wheelock.

"Oh, I doubt it was that," Rita replied quickly, refusing to admit the need of a defense against Winifred—or was it Dolly? Which one it was she couldn't bear thinking about at all. "It probably had more to do with being hungry when she got home after I'd gone to bed. She said she looked at the leftover roast beef in the refrigerator and thought about making herself a sandwich but didn't want to bother."

"Hunger can bring on bad dreams," Mrs. Wheelock conceded.

"That would explain the knife, wouldn't it—making herself a sandwich?"

"I suppose so," the older woman said but her tone lacked conviction. "I still don't like it and I'm sure you don't either."

"Nor Winifred."

"Of course not. But it's you I'm concerned about, Rita, alone here with a woman who sleepwalks and gets out knives. It could be dangerous."

"I realize that and so does Winifred. She was more worried about it than I was."

"Did she offer to leave?"

Silence from Rita, then reluctantly, "Yes."

"What did you say?"

Rita sighed to herself knowing that she couldn't overlook this chance to start letting go of Winifred. But her tone was still reluctant as she replied, "I told her to take her time over it."

"Meanwhile, though, there's no guarantee it won't happen again. I'd be scared stiff if it happened to anyone living with me."

"I was. I didn't tell Winifred that. She was scared enough herself, as it was. I just looked through some old keys and found one that fitted my bedroom door. I said if it would make her feel better, I'd lock myself in at night."

"That's all right as a temporary measure. You can't keep it up, though, locking yourself in against a sleepwalking roommate."

"But at least it takes immediate pressure off Winifred to leave," Rita pointed out.

"It's not solving any of her problems, however." Mrs. Wheelock paused in thought. "Perhaps she should see a psychiatrist."

"Mrs. Wheelock!" Rita protested indignantly. "She's perfectly sane. As sane as either one of us."

"Now Rita, that's an outdated attitude to take toward psychiatric help. Lots of people turn to it when they're faced with problems they can't handle alone."

"Well, I certainly couldn't suggest it to Winifred."

"I guess not. But why does the idea of it upset you so much?"

Rita shrugged off the question. "I just don't like it, that's all."

Did it cut too close to the bone? Mrs. Wheelock wondered. Rita might long ago have benefited from psychiatric help herself; might still, for that matter. And be aware of this need somewhere inside her.

On the other hand, her reaction might be based on nothing more than the realization that she had been too hasty in letting Winifred come to live with her and now did not want to admit that she had made a mistake.

That was the end of conversation about Winifred. But on the way home Mrs. Wheelock thought about the emotional crisis her behavior indicated and that it was too bad that Rita, who had problems enough of her own, had ever got involved with her.

But it just wasn't in Rita to tell her to leave. Anyone who didn't know they had scraped up acquaintance in a restaurant and become roommates only about a month ago would assume that Winifred was an old friend to whom Rita owed great loyalty.

Mrs. Wheelock, in a situation where she had to lock her bedroom door at night to feel safe, wouldn't put up with it for a minute.

But that was what Rita was doing. Was the poor girl so in need of companionship that she would accept it on any terms?

Apparently. And all over Ted Parker. Look at the terrible state she had got into when he dropped her for that wretched Janet, not just over losing him but because she saw him as the end of the line where her prospects of marriage were concerned. The short time they had gone out together didn't come into the picture; it was the importance she attached to keeping him that had done her so much damage.

The saddest part of it was that she might still be seeing him if only she had been a little less eager, less obvious in pursuing the man or rather, the dream he represented.

There would still, of course, have been Janet.

No, not necessarily. If Rita hadn't always been pushing things, arranging dates with Ted Parker, he and Janet might never have met.

But Rita, having learned nothing from past failures, had gone right ahead almost, it seemed, reaching out to embrace her latest one.

It was unfortunate, though, that while the pain of it was still so sharp, Winifred Lawton had come into her life.

At another time, when she wasn't so unhappy herself, Rita might have been less ready to take a comparative stranger into her house. Or at least, with Winifred going her own way, giving Rita little of the friendship she sought, she might now have found it easier to ask her to leave.

Did she hesitate because she was actually afraid—or, if not that, a little in awe of Winifred?

There was no answer to that question. It was just another facet of Rita's relationship with Winifred that was becoming more and more of an enigma to Mrs. Wheelock. And even, on Rita's behalf, a source of uneasiness.

If she herself could only get the chance to meet Winifred, she reflected, she would at least be able to form her own opinion of her.

Rita, however, seemed to be in no hurry to bring a meeting about—or was it Winifred, keeping her distance, who was responsible for that?

Either way, Mrs. Wheelock could hardly force the issue.

While Rita was getting ready for bed that night she heard a car approaching. Was it Winifred?

She shook off the involuntary thought as no more than a repetition of the peculiar moment on the patio when she could almost see Winifred in the kitchen with a knife in her hand. She had talked too much about her today to Mrs. Wheelock, that was the trouble.

Rita got into bed forgetting to lock the door.

Later, though, drifting off to sleep, some small sound downstairs brought her wide awake. She sat up and listened but did not hear it again. Just the house cooling off at night. She had often heard the same sort of sound before.

As she settled back on her pillow, however, her glance fell on the dark oblong of the doorway that seemed to invite someone to appear in it.

She sprang out of bed and closed and locked the door.

After that she went right to sleep.

XVII

Janet was at loose ends just then, working the second shift at the hospital and finding no great demand for her company nights that she was free. Ted Parker was still in North Carolina and Sam Richards' off-duty hours rarely of late coincided with hers. There was a promising newcomer in the next apartment but they were only beginning to get acquainted and she couldn't look to him yet to enliven her social life.

And so, with time on her hands, Janet devoted more and more idle moments to the mystery connected with Winifred that made Rita turn down every suggestion for meeting her.

What had begun as mere curiosity on Janet's part had grown with her conviction that there was something peculiar going on and had now reached the point where she decided she would try to circumvent Rita and bring about a meeting on her own.

She considered ways and means of accomplishing it.

Not through another phone call to Rita who would only turn her down again and who probably hadn't even mentioned Janet's earlier invitation to Winifred. A phone call then to Winifred herself at The Blue Grotto? No, that wouldn't do when they were perfect strangers to each other. She could, of course, drop in at Rita's in the hope of catching Winifred home; but if she wasn't there it was wasted effort and could only be tried once, the way Rita was acting.

There must be some way to handle it. But how?

A new approach came to her one night at the hospital. It

came during a lull at her station with visiting hours over, patients settled for the night.

Why not, she thought, call Rita's number and ask for
Winifred? Or rather, have someone else, whose voice would be
unfamiliar if Rita answered the phone, make the call for her.

If Winifred was home Janet would chat a little—"It's just
hopeless trying to get Rita to bring you over so I thought I'd
invite you myself—"

Much better to do it that way than to call Winifred at work.

All she needed was someone obliging who would accept a
simple explanation for what she wanted done and whose voice
would sound completely different from hers on the phone.

In the end she approached one of the nurse's aides, an
easygoing girl with a deep voice that was sometimes mistaken
for a man's.

"Do me a favor?" she asked.

"Sure. What is it?"

"Call this number for me." Janet handed her a slip of paper
with Rita's phone number on it. "I want to speak to someone
there but I don't want to call myself in case this other girl I'm
not friendly with answers."

"Oh." The aide reached for the phone on the desk. "Who
shall I ask for?"

"Winifred Lawton. If she answers herself, hand me the
phone quick like a bunny rabbit. If the other girl answers and
says Winifred's not home, ask what time she's expected."

"Okay. Then what?"

"Just hang up."

"No message or anything?"

"Nothing. Just hang up."

The aide dialed the number and when Rita answered said,
"I'd like to speak to Winifred Lawton, please."

There was a moment of dead silence from Rita. Her flesh
crept. Then she managed to reply, "Winifred isn't home."

"What time do you expect her?"

Was it a man's voice or a woman's?

Rita tried to keep her own voice steady. "She's working to-night and won't be home until late. Who shall I say called?"

But even as she asked this the phone was hung up.

"Well, that's it," the aide said to Janet. "Winifred's working tonight and won't be home until late."

"Thanks, anyway, for making the call."

"You're welcome." The aide left.

Working late, thought Janet. That meant Winifred would sleep late tomorrow morning.

Janet herself, not getting home much before midnight, wouldn't be getting up early either. But she could make it a point to be up by nine o'clock or so when Rita would be safely off to work.

Why hadn't she thought of doing it before?

Rita had answered on the upstairs phone in her room. Dark terrors shook her as she hung up and sank down on the bed rubbing the gooseflesh that still prickled her arms.

That voice asking matter-of-factly for Winifred as if she might answer the phone, as if she were real, as if she lived in this house. . . .

Rita's glance probed every corner of the room as if she herself expected Winifred to appear, to take on substance.

But she didn't exist.

And yet there had been that voice on the phone asking to speak to her.

Ancient evils—Black Masses, witches' Sabbaths, sorcerers' rites, a jumble of barely remembered tales swirled through Rita's mind. But they dealt with lost souls, raising the dead, casting spells—and none of this could apply to Winifred.

Who didn't exist.

Then, as the first shock faded, common sense asserted itself. Whoever had called, man or woman—it didn't matter which— had no supernatural connections, had, in fact, been given some reason to believe that there was a Winifred Lawton living in this house.

Only two people, Mrs. Wheelock and Janet, knew that there was supposed to be such a person.

Mrs. Wheelock could be eliminated immediately as a party to the phone call. That left Janet—and whoever she had talked to about Winifred.

Janet, then, had staged the whole thing, getting the other person to make the call for her, inventing some plausible reason for not making it herself.

How maddeningly persistent she was about Winifred!

A spasm of rage swept Rita. How was she going to get that nosy little bitch off her back? There must be a way even though none occurred to her at the moment.

Talk it over with Mrs. Wheelock?

Of course not. She could hardly admit that there was no one in the world except Janet who would call Winifred.

At least Janet didn't know the call had scared Rita half to death.

On her way to bed that night Rita paused in the doorway to Winifred's room. The mirror on the opposite wall gave back her reflection, her face in shadow but the light behind her in the hall casting a reddish glow on her dark hair.

For a heart-stopping moment she seemed to be Winifred.

Janet waited until nine-thirty the next morning to call Winifred, giving her time to catch up on her sleep. With her finger hovering over the dial she rehearsed her side of the conversation.

She would ask for Rita. When Winifred replied that Rita had left for work Janet would say, Already? It's only eight-thirty and it doesn't take her long to get there.

Winifred would look at her bedside clock and say, No, it's nine-thirty.

Janet would laugh. Is it? Heavens, I'm way behind this morning. Then she would add, You must be Winifred, Rita's roommate.

Yes, Winifred would say.

Janet would then introduce herself. I'm Janet Murray, a

friend of Rita's. She's often mentioned you since you moved in with her. I wonder if she's ever said that I'd like to meet you? Or that I suggested she bring you over some evening to have a drink with me?

At that point improvisation had to end. What followed next would depend on Winifred's response.

Janet dialed the number. She let it ring and ring but all that came of it was the echoing sound of an empty house.

She felt a sense of letdown when she hung up. She had waited too long. Winifred, in spite of working late, was already up and dressed and gone.

Not to go to work this early, though. A shopping trip? A dentist appointment?

Janet tried the number again at eleven, at noon and for the last time just before she left for work herself.

Funny, she thought. Well, maybe not. Winifred had probably made plans that were keeping her away all day.

Try again tomorrow. Try a little earlier, soon after nine o'clock.

By Friday of that week, after three days of trying to reach Winifred at varying hours between nine and five when Rita wouldn't be home, Janet didn't know what to make of it. Unless, she thought, Winifred, having worked the first part of the week had taken the rest of it off and gone away somewhere.

No use trying to reach her over the weekend when Rita would be home. But if she was away, she surely would be home next week.

Janet would have to catch her then because the following week on her rotating schedule she would be back on the first shift. The coming weekend she would be away herself, going home to Granville over Memorial Day, a trip she had been postponing for various reasons since Easter.

Monday morning, running through her rehearsed speech again—although she practically knew it by heart at that point— Janet tried once more to call Winifred. She kept trying the number at intervals until it was time for her to go to work. With no response that day or the next she felt more at a loss than ever. It just wasn't possible, she thought, for Winifred to be away or working every time Janet had tried to call her.

What else then?

One answer might be that Winifred had moved out since Janet had last called Rita. She hadn't mentioned it but then she was so closemouthed anyway where Winifred was concerned that Janet could never get her to say much about her. On the other hand, if Rita knew Winifred was leaving soon, it gave her a good excuse, which she hadn't taken advantage of, for turning down Janet's invitation.

Instead, she had just talked about how busy Winifred was and said she didn't know when she could bring her over.

Maybe it had all happened since. Maybe Winifred had got so fed up with Rita—like that other girl, Louise Brooks—that she had just moved out overnight too.

There was satisfaction in thinking that this was what had happened. It would serve Rita right for being so snippy about a get-together at Janet's, acting as if Winifred were royalty or something.

On her way to work Janet decided to call Rita from the hospital. She could say she was going to Granville for the weekend and ask if Rita had anything she wanted to send home to her parents. Then she could bring up Winifred.

What story would Rita tell to account for Winifred's leaving?

If she had left. But she must have. Otherwise, she would certainly have been home at least once out of the many times Janet had tried to reach her.

Rita gave her little information, however, when she called her that night. No, she said, there wasn't anything she wanted to send to her parents. She didn't even sound particularly pleased over what should have seemed a thoughtful gesture on Janet's part.

"I just thought there might be," Janet said.

"No, not a thing."

"Busy as ever these days, Rita?"

"Oh yes."

"And Winifred?"

"She's very busy too." Rita's tone was designed to cut off any renewal of Janet's invitation that she bring Winifred over for a drink.

Janet made no mention of it. "I'd better get back to work now," she said.

"Have a nice trip," Rita said.

"I'm sure I will. 'By for now."

"Good-by."

That was that, Rita thought hanging up. Apparently Janet had at last got the message that it would do her no good to keep pushing to meet Winifred.

Janet herself hung up in puzzlement. Winifred had not moved out after all.

And yet she was never home no matter what odd hour Janet tried to reach her. There was something awfully funny about it. Something weird.

Janet made a few more attempts to call Winifred during the next few days.

How could she be out all the time? Janet asked herself exasperatedly after her last futile call. What could be going on with her?

Whatever it was, Rita was at the bottom of it. But if she thought she was going to get away with it, she was very much mistaken.

Janet tossed her ash-blond head to emphasize for her own benefit how firm she was in her intention not to let Rita put anything over on her.

XVIII

When Janet got home that weekend she learned that there was a package at the house for her to take back to Rita.

"From her aunt Mary," Janet's mother said. "I ran into her after church Sunday and when I mentioned that you'd be home this weekend she asked if you'd mind taking Rita's birthday present back with you. Her birthday is almost a month off so there's no hurry about delivering it or having her pick it up. But it's a lot easier to send it with you than to wrap it for mailing. You don't mind, do you?"

"No, not at all," Janet replied, privately enjoying the irony of it, her excuse for calling Rita the other night turned into reality except that the package would go in the opposite direction.

"It's a flame-stitch pillow," her mother continued. "Rita's in luck with the beautiful handiwork her aunt does. I would've loved to have seen it but it was gift-wrapped when she brought it over. Rita will probably show it to you, though."

"Yes," said Janet knowing she would pick her own time for dropping the birthday present off at Rita's. Her twenty-ninth birthday, wasn't it? And no husband in sight.

Poor old Rita. Janet smiled to herself.

She got back to Falls Church late that Monday night and set her alarm for quarter of six so as to be at the hospital by seven o'clock the next morning. It was the shift she liked best. It meant that her evenings were free again. And this week Sam would have some nights off too.

Another bright spot was that Ted Parker would be returning

soon from North Carolina. He took her to more expensive places than Sam or anyone else she knew could afford.

Still, she should broaden her field. How about her new neighbor? It was time she made some casual move in his direction.

On that thought Janet went to sleep.

She had a date with Sam Richards Wednesday night. Nothing to get excited about, she reflected, getting dressed for it. They were to pick up Sam's former roommate who lived on Wisconsin Avenue and then stop for his girl. The four of them would have dinner somewhere, not any special place, and go to a movie afterward.

Putting on her make-up, the thought came to her that when Ted got back she would suggest The Blue Grotto for dinner. To celebrate his return, she would say; and so, at least get a look at Winifred. Unless she wasn't working that night.

That was a chance Janet would have to take.

Half an hour later, driving across the Roosevelt Bridge with Sam Richards, she had another inspiration. She looked at her watch and said, "Know what? We're a little early. Why don't we stop somewhere for a drink before we pick up Walter? He's always late anyway. Worse than I am."

"Well, just one," Sam replied. "Where do you want to go?"

"How about The Blue Grotto?"

"Hey, you're flying high, girl. That place costs an arm and a leg just to walk through the door."

"Oh, come on, not for a drink. One of the nurses who was there recently said it was a great place to go."

"Well, okay. But just one drink, remember. I'm kind of hard up this week."

There was a parking lot for patrons next to The Blue Grotto. Sam left his car there, pocketed a check stub from the attendant, and they went inside, into a carpeted lobby with lush growing plants and muted blue lights playing on a tank of brilliantly colored tropical fish.

The dining room, still empty at this hour but with tables laid for dinner lay straight ahead through an open archway. To their right a discreet sign said "Cocktail Lounge."

A hostess materialized out of the dimness as they went in. "Two?" she asked.

"Yes."

She seated them at a small corner table, Janet dismissing her after a glance. She was tall, good-looking, dark-haired. Not Winifred. Neither was the only other hostess in sight, equally tall but as blond as Janet herself.

Was height a qualification for the job? How tall was Winifred?

A waiter took their order. Their drinks were served accompanied by a dish of salted almonds.

"I'll take my time with this," Janet dimpled as she picked up her glass. "I know it's got to last."

"It sure has." Sam helped himself to a handful of almonds and tasted his martini. "Perfect," he said. "I wonder if the food here is this good too."

More people came in and were seated by the two hostesses. Still no Winifred.

Not working tonight, Janet reflected disappointedly. Or coming on duty a little later?

No, not that. The cocktail lounge was filling up, early diners would begin to appear soon. Winifred must have the night off.

They lingered over their drinks until their waiter started to eye them inquiringly. Then Sam asked for the check, paid it and said, "Guess I'll use the men's room before we leave. You want to go to the women's and meet me in the lobby?"

Janet shook her head, her gaze moving past him to the dark-haired hostess who was seating a group nearby, offering an opportunity not to be missed. "I'll wait for you here," she said.

When the group was seated she beckoned to the hostess.

"Yes?" the latter said halting beside her table.

She looked so aloof that Janet felt it necessary to display her dimple ingratiatingly. "Could you tell me, please, if Winifred Lawton is working tonight?"

"Winifred Lawton?" An eyebrow was raised. "Working here, you mean?"

"Yes. She's a hostess here too. She lives with a friend of

mine and I just thought I'd introduce myself—" Janet broke off in uncertainty.

"Winifred Lawton." The hostess shook her head. "She doesn't work here."

"She's given up her job?"

"No, not that. There's been no one named Winifred Lawton here since I came two years ago. You must have it mixed up with some other restaurant."

"Oh . . ." Janet's voice trailed off. "That must be it."

"And now if you'll excuse me—"

"Yes, of course. Thanks a lot."

The hostess moved away.

Janet still looked so bemused when Sam returned that he asked, "What's the matter?"

"Nothing." She brought her faraway gaze into focus on him.

"Don't give me that."

"Well, as a matter of fact, I was thinking about a dress I saw in a store yesterday. Couldn't afford it."

"That all? I'll buy it for you—when I get rich."

They went out to Sam's car. Which one, Winifred or Rita, had lied about The Blue Grotto? Janet asked herself on the way. Either Winifred had lied to Rita about where she worked or Rita had lied about it to Janet. It was as simple as that.

For the rest of the evening the question weighed on Janet's mind; but it wasn't until she was home getting ready for bed that she could give her full attention to it.

She began with the few facts Rita had supplied on Winifred.

Very attractive, she had said the day she first mentioned her to Janet. That much at least was true. Judging by her picture, Winifred was perfectly stunning.

Divorcee? Janet would accept that too. There'd be no reason to lie about it, a side issue.

Winifred and Rita weren't old friends. They'd only met last fall, Rita had said. Was it true? Probably. There'd be no reason to lie about that either.

There was, in fact, only one lie that Janet could pin down: Winifred did not work at The Blue Grotto.

But which one had lied about it, Winifred herself or Rita?

Back to square one, Janet thought impatiently, putting on her nightgown. If only she knew more about Rita's friendship with Winifred, how close they were, how much they told each other about themselves! But there'd been no way to find out with Rita acting so snippy about Winifred right from the start.

Why?

She shrugged off the question. It was Rita's nature, that was all. She wasn't easy to get along with. She went around with a chip on her shoulder most of the time.

It didn't enter Janet's mind that there might be something personal in Rita's hostility toward her. Everyone else, particularly men, liked her, didn't they? She had no off-putting personality quirks like Rita's, she would have said. She could get along with almost anybody and had never, so far as she knew, made an enemy in her life.

A little later, smoothing out her unmade bed before she got into it, Janet decided that on balance, she was inclined to believe that it was Winifred who had lied about The Blue Grotto.

If it had been Rita, Janet thought, she would have come up with something better where Winifred's job was concerned. Being a hostess, even in a plush restaurant, wasn't all that great really when it came to being a status thing.

Which meant, Janet thought, settling down in bed, that Rita hadn't known Winifred very well at the time they became roommates. Rattling around alone in her house, she had just grabbed at the first chance she got to have someone move in with her.

It took Janet a while to go to sleep. She had a new question to ponder. If Winifred was the one who had lied about where she worked, what reason did she have for it?

Something shady, something crooked about her real job?

A call girl, for instance?

No. She'd want her own apartment for that.

Some kind of undercover job for the FBI, maybe, or the CIA?

That possibility fascinated Janet. But it wouldn't stand up. Anything like that, she reminded herself, Winifred would be given better cover so that the first person who asked about her at The Blue Grotto, as Janet had, wouldn't be told that she didn't work there.

What else could it be?

Something crooked . . .

Drug traffic? No, because that would mean being part of an organization and for that too she would have good cover.

What in the world could it be?

Go back to hostess. That much about her job could be true. Something outside the law, though.

Gambling joint? Was that illegal in Washington?

Janet didn't know. But probably, she thought. It didn't seem like the sort of thing that would be accepted in the nation's capital.

So that might be it. Janet, drawing on old TV movies she had seen, pictured Winifred in long slinky dresses, red hair piled high on her head, shoulders bare, moving among gaming tables patronized by men in evening clothes. The setting would be some secluded mansion that would provide discreet parking out in back for Cadillacs and Lincolns, Mercedes, Jaguars and Porsches, maybe even a Rolls or two. . . .

Her eyes closed. Tomorrow, she told herself drifting off to sleep, she would think about it some more.

XIX

The mystery posed by Winifred was never far from Janet's thoughts the next day. It came and went through her mind, a challenge she couldn't let alone.

She was going out again that night with Sam Richards who was due at eight o'clock. At seven-thirty, giving herself plenty of time to talk, she called Rita.

It really would be something, she thought dialing the number, if just this once Winifred was home and answered the phone. Janet wished she would but then had second thoughts as it started to ring. She wouldn't be able to tell Rita what she had found out last night if Winifred was around.

So it was just as well that Rita was the one who answered the phone.

"Hi," Janet said. "It's me."

"Yes?"

That neutral tone again. What a difficult type Rita was! No wonder she turned men off.

"I called to let you know that I have a package here for you from Granville."

"Oh?"

"A birthday present from your aunt Mary. She gave it to my mother for me to bring back to you. But I'm not to be in any hurry giving it to you, your aunt said. Not until it's nearer your birthday."

"Well, in that case, why don't I call you a little later on?"

Rita suggested. "Then we'll work out a time when you'll be home for me to pick it up."

"Now Rita, you shouldn't have to come and get your own birthday present." Janet giggled as she added, "But don't expect me to sing 'Happy Birthday' when I deliver it to you."

When you come snooping again, Rita thought in vexation, and then, But you're not going to get away with it, poking around my house again trying to find out more about Winifred.

What she would have to do, she thought next, was forestall Janet. Make sure she was home some night well in advance of her birthday and arrive unannounced to pick up her present.

"We needn't worry about when I'm to get it just yet," she said. "But thanks for calling and letting me know—and also for bringing it back with you."

She was ready to hang up.

"Oh, one more thing," Janet said hurriedly. "It's sort of peculiar really . . ."

"Yes?"

"I had a date last night with Sam—you know, Sam Richards? —and we went to The Blue Grotto—"

"How nice," said Rita with no trace of the dismay she felt in her voice but with her mind racing ahead to find an answer to what she knew was coming next.

"—and I got into a conversation with the hostess who seated us. You know what she said when I asked her if Winifred was there?"

"What?"

"She said she didn't work there. Imagine!" Janet sounded breathless with amazement.

Rita could almost see her at the moment, eyes bright over the prospect of stirring up trouble.

"The hostess said she hadn't worked there, either, not during the past two years. What do you suppose it means, Rita? Why should she say she did?"

"I have no idea."

"You don't sound surprised."

"Of course I am!"

"I can't get over it myself. It's the weirdest thing I ever heard of, telling you a story like that, when you're close friends and she's living in your house."

Rita picked up the lead Janet was giving her. "Not that close friends," she said.

"Oh?" Janet's tone was all innocence. "I guess I just took it for granted—"

"You always do that," Rita retorted. "It's a bad habit, one you should break. I told you I met Winifred only a few months ago. We became friends right away, though, and began getting together now and then. She didn't like the place where she was living so I let her come here. That's all there is to it."

"Except that she lied to you about where she worked," Janet pointed out.

"No doubt she had her reasons."

"I'm sure she had. What I think myself is that if she's a hostess anywhere, it's in some shady place like a gambling joint or something like that."

"Well," Rita said startled but relieved that this was Janet's view of it. And after a moment, "Pretty farfetched, isn't it? There could be a much simpler explanation for the whole thing."

"I must say you take it calmly enough. I'd be a lot more concerned if I were in your shoes."

"I don't see why. It's up to her, isn't it, where she wants to say she works?"

"Maybe. But how about—?" Janet, annoyed that Rita was taking her news so calmly, stopped herself just in time from saying that wherever Winifred worked, she could never be reached at home. There was no way to bring that in without admitting how often she had tried to call her while Rita was at work herself.

"How about what?"

"I was just wondering if you're going to ask Winifred why she lied to you about The Blue Grotto."

"I'll have to think about it first," Rita replied abruptly, anger rising in her now that she had dealt with Janet's revelation.

Why should she put up with any more of her insufferable prying? "It's her business," she added freezingly. "Maybe mine. But not yours, Janet. No way at all."

"Heaven's sake," Janet protested on an injured note. "I just thought as a friend of yours that you'd want to know."

"Friend of mine? Well, call it what you like. I've got to go now. Good-by." Rita hung up.

Janet gasped as the bang of the receiver hit her ear. What did Rita mean by that last crack of hers? What was the matter with her anyway? She hadn't even thanked Janet for trying to do her a favor.

In righteous indignation Janet had no trouble persuading herself that she had made the call from the best of intentions.

Rita's fantasy took a different form. The anger that consumed her brought her to the verge of calling The Blue Grotto to tell Winifred what Janet had said. But she checked herself as she started to reach for the phone book to look up the number. What was she thinking of, lapsing once again into almost believing that Winifred was real?

She had to stop it. There was no Winifred. She didn't exist.

Rita fled outdoors to the patio where she had been reading the evening paper when Janet called.

She picked it up but couldn't concentrate on what she read. Presently she laid it aside and gave herself up to the tranquil approach of night, watching colors fade from her flowers, birds taking a last drink of water from the birdbath, splashing it out on the grass.

A crescent moon rose in the east. It was a beautiful May night, a night to bring a lift to the most troubled spirits.

Except that she couldn't stay out there forever. Bedtime came and she had to go indoors to face it.

She went reluctantly, fearful of the nightmares and sleepwalking that had followed on other calls from Janet, that thorn in her side, that festering sore. Janet, who wouldn't stay out of her life.

With a great effort of will Rita put her out of her mind as she went upstairs.

She turned on the light in Winifred's room before she went into her own. The flowers on the desk were past their prime. Sometime tomorrow she would cut fresh ones.

"Good night, Winifred," she said and turned out the light.

In spite of the fears that hung over her at bedtime, Rita, locking her door, slept peacefully through the night.

Neither Winifred nor Janet was on her mind the next morning driving to work. Instead, her thoughts were on the date she had that night with an underwriter from the home office. She had met him at the agency and whenever he was in the area, usually three or four times a year, he took her out to dinner. She enjoyed the expense-account lavishness of going out with him but from the first had recognized that their association would never go beyond that. He was in his forties, divorced, and fixed in his intention not to remarry.

Nevertheless, a date with him was something to look forward to.

She discussed it with Mrs. Wheelock at lunch, still giving no thought to Winifred or Janet.

Then, from out of the blue, she heard herself say, "Janet called last night to tell me she'd been to The Blue Grotto."

"Really?" Mrs. Wheelock smiled. "I'm sure she made it a point to introduce herself to Winifred. She'd never let a chance like that go by."

"No, of course not. She couldn't though because—" Rita broke off just short of telling the older woman the whole story of what Janet had said. She substituted hurriedly, "Winifred wasn't there."

"That must have been a disappointment. Was Winifred home last night when Janet called?"

"No. She was working."

"So Janet missed the boat the night before." Mrs. Wheelock nodded in satisfaction. "It's too bad, though, that she won't stop making a nuisance of herself."

"Yes . . ." Rita spoke in a preoccupied tone. There was no reason whatsoever for her to have had another of those curious little lapses over Winifred.

She tried to listen and laugh in the right places as Mrs.
Wheelock told her about a phone call that morning from a
policyholder with a dubious claim. But in another part of her
mind she remained in a small state of shock over her latest
lapse.

What had struck her that she had suddenly started to tell
Mrs. Wheelock what Janet had really said last night?

It wasn't as if there had first been some mention of Janet or
Winifred; or as if Rita herself at the moment had been thinking about the call.

There had been nothing like that. For no reason at all, there
had come to her the sudden need to talk about it, to share the
whole thing with Mrs. Wheelock, particularly Janet's prepos-
terous suggestion that Winifred worked in a gambling joint.

Mrs. Wheelock, though, would have brushed that part aside
to fasten on the fact that Winifred had lied about her job, and
would, of course, have been more concerned than ever that
Rita still wasn't pressing her to leave.

Only yesterday Mrs. Wheelock had asked if Winifred was
looking for another place.

"Oh yes," Rita had replied. "But she hasn't found anything
that suits her yet."

What would Mrs. Wheelock's reaction have been to the real
story of why Janet had called?

That was beside the point, actually. Rita's main concern was
that she'd had another of those lapses. It was a warning signal
that she had already played her silly game far too long; that she
really had to let go of Winifred, could not go on putting it off.
It was senseless, stupid. She had to ignore the familiar sinking
feeling that came at the prospect of it.

Winifred did not exist.

XX

The weekend, bringing in June, flew by for Rita. There was her dinner date Friday night. Saturday she shopped, worked outdoors and went to a movie in the evening with a friend. Sunday she entertained the Hunts and their widower neighbor at a cookout.

She stayed outside on the patio after they left enjoying the quiet night fragrant with the scent of her roses, looking up at the sky to seek out stars she recognized. Her mind was virtually empty of thought until Dolly took possession of it.

"Oh no," she said and got to her feet. She walked back and forth across the lawn trying to think of something else, anything at all that would blank her sister out of her memory.

Sometimes she could. Not always, though. Not, she realized in despair, tonight. Tonight she could not stop herself from reliving the tragedy of Dolly's death from the beginning to the sad and terrible conclusion.

Looking at the stars had brought it on, Rita thought, as she went slowly back to her chair. The night before Dolly died their father had taken them for a walk before bedtime and had pointed out stars he was familiar with as they looked up at the sky. A September sky that night, Dolly running ahead, Rita walking sedately beside him.

Dolly was running in most of Rita's memories of her. Light as a feather, she seemed to skim over the ground barely touching it, always in a hurry, reaching out for whatever lay ahead, the day itself, a special treat, a game, a toy, a friend.

Could she somehow have sensed how short her life would be and that she must make the most of every moment of it?

That last afternoon she had been eager to play their new game of thwarting bank robbers, getting back the money that had been stolen and becoming famous themselves through their achievement.

Rita had invented the game straight out of the pages of Nancy Drew.

Dolly, who could whistle better than Rita, imitated the approach of the train while Rita chuffed and puffed to convey its halt at the barricade.

As the inventor of the game she assigned herself the role of stalking the robbers through the train leaving Dolly to wait beside the tracks for the money to be dropped out a window.

But that last afternoon she got impatient standing around as Rita prolonged the drama of her stalking. When the latter finally tossed the pocketbook to her, Dolly, in a perverse mood, opened it and took out the play money instead of running back among the trees with it as she was supposed to do.

Her hands were too small to hold it all. She dropped a large part of it and there was just enough wind to blow it in every direction.

"Look what you've done, you stupid idiot," Rita screamed at her from the middle of the tracks. "Pick it all up now."

Dolly stumbled around frantically scooping it up, shoving it back into the pocketbook with Rita, who refused to help her—it was Dolly's own fault, wasn't it?—shouting instructions.

"There's one you missed over by that bush—no, dummy, the other bush! Hey, get that one over there by the ravine before it blows into it!"

Dolly, not her usual light-footed self, hampered by high heels and her mother's dress tripping her up, broke into a wobbly run in pursuit of the green piece of paper fluttering toward the edge of the ravine.

Just then another piece landed at Rita's feet and she deigned to bend over and pick it up. There was a fleeting moment when her eyes weren't on Dolly and that was the moment when she fell into the ravine.

She screamed wildly again and again as she bounced from rock to rock down the almost perpendicular drop, the last echoes of her screams ending in sudden terrifying silence.

Rita ran, stumbled, kicked off her own high heels, ran faster to the edge of the ravine. She couldn't even see Dolly at first, half-hidden as she was by underbrush at the bottom, but then her frenzied gaze picked out the small still figure.

Dolly lay face down among the rocks and for a moment Rita thought that she moved. But it was only a tatter of their mother's new green dress lifted by the wind.

Rita's immediate panicky reaction was to the ruin of the dress. Their mother would be so mad and would blame her because she was older and should have stopped Dolly from taking it.

Sitting there on the patio, eyes wet with tears, Rita still found it hard to believe that the ruined dress had been her first reaction to the tragedy. There was no way to get back into her eight-year-old mind, to reconstruct her thoughts at the time. They had only added to the burden of guilt she had carried ever since.

"Dolly," she called over and over. "Dolly!" No answer came.

Except to fall like Dolly, there was no way to reach her sister.

At last she began to cry. Dolly didn't move or speak because she was dead. Rita in her rage, sending her after that last piece of play money, had killed her.

Dolly had always been a little afraid of Rita when she went into one of her rages. Dolly . . .

How long did she kneel there staring down at the small still figure?

At last she picked up the pocketbook, her dress-up shoes and fled.

The new green dress. Their mother would be so mad. . . .

Rita got up and walked back and forth across the lawn again.

It did no good. Back in her chair she still had to face all that followed thereafter.

Five o'clock that afternoon. She had got home, tiptoed up the stairs, put away the dress-ups, and was curled up with a book in her room before her mother appeared and asked, "Where's Dolly?"

"She's out back," Rita said, heart pounding.

"No, she isn't. I just looked. I thought you were both out there."

"She was when I came in."

"What was she doing?"

"She was on the swing. She wanted me to push her some more but I said no." (Always elaborations on lies seemed to have been part of Rita's life.)

"Well, I'll go call her again."

Their mother didn't realize they had left the yard; she had been too busy with her canning to check on them.

Rita could hear her calling from the back door. There could be no answer. Dolly was dead. No amount of calling would bring her back.

Rita heard her mother open the front door, step out on the front porch, not worried yet, looking up and down the street, probably, as she went on calling. She heard her father's car drive in, her mother asking if he had seen Dolly anywhere on his way home.

Rita hung over the banister and listened to the discussion that followed. The first note of worry came into their voices, mingled with annoyance that Dolly had gone off somewhere by herself without permission.

Presently, Rita was summoned downstairs by her father.

"Your mother says you and Dolly went outdoors to play around three o'clock," he began. "Did you stay in the yard the whole time?"

It was a big yard and out in back where they played was mostly screened from view by trees and shrubbery. It was safe to say yes to that question.

"You didn't see Dolly again after you came in the house yourself?"

"Not exactly," Rita replied. "But she came in a few minutes after I did. Mama was still canning in the kitchen. She had the radio on so I guess she didn't hear her. Dolly came upstairs and went in your room. She only stayed in there about a minute and then went back downstairs and outdoors again."

(That covered the green dress and high-heeled shoes.)

"You didn't talk to her at all?"

"No, I was in my room reading."

Rita's father looked at his watch and frowned. "It's twenty minutes to six," he said to her mother. "Where would she go this near suppertime?"

"I can't imagine. I don't like it. It's getting chilly too. The paper said rain tonight and there's Dolly off somewhere in her playclothes, not even a sweater on." Rita's mother paused, then said, "Why don't you take the car and go look for her?"

"That's a good idea." Rita's father headed for the door. "Meanwhile, you start calling people."

"Right away." Rita's mother went to the phone saying half to herself, "Let's see, who shall I start with?"

"Judy Barrett's her best friend," Rita offered. (Why had she said that, haunted as she was by the image of the small still figure almost hidden from sight at the bottom of the ravine? Had she thought that mentioning Judy Barrett would make it go away? Or was she just trying to remove herself still farther from any knowledge of it?)

Her mother called Judy Barrett and then other friends of Dolly's beginning with those who lived closest by. When the list of friends was exhausted she moved on to neighbors.

Rita's father broke in once calling to ask if Dolly had come home yet and saying he would keep on looking himself.

"Aunt Mary?" Rita suggested at one point.

"It's two miles away. She'd call right away if Dolly showed up there." But then Rita's mother called her anyway.

By the time Rita's father returned it was nearly seven o'clock and her aunt Mary and uncle Roger were on their way over. Her mother was now reduced to calling mere acquaintances.

Rita made herself small in a corner while the adults conferred and a few more calls were made. Supper had been forgotten. She couldn't have eaten in any case. Her stomach was tied up in a hard knot.

Her uncle Roger turned to her. "What time did you come in the house after you played outside this afternoon?" he asked.

"I don't know. I didn't look at the clock. But maybe about half an hour before Mama asked me where Dolly was."

"That was a little after five," Rita's mother said.

"Why did you both use the front door going back and forth? Don't you use the back door most of the time?"

"Yes, but Mama was canning all afternoon and didn't want us underfoot in the kitchen."

Uncle Roger looked at his watch. "Quarter past seven. Dolly's been missing nearly three hours now."

"Too long for a six-year-old," Rita's father said. "Almost dark now and rain due any minute. I'm going to call the police."

By eight o'clock with the warm September day turning into a cold rainy night, the house was filled with police and neighbors gathering to join the search party.

It was years before Rita was old enough to understand the special note in lowered voices talking about the possibility of some man having taken Dolly off in his car. Her father's tight-lipped look, her mother's tears conveyed no particular meaning to her then.

It was raining hard when Aunt Mary finally took Rita up to bed and brought her cereal and milk. But she could not eat.

Or sleep when she was alone in her room. She dozed uneasily at intervals but kept coming awake to the sound of voices downstairs and rain beating on the windows, beating on Dolly's body there in the ravine.

At some point during the endless night she heard dogs barking outside. What did they want with dogs? After a moment of taut listening she realized that it was to help in the search for Dolly. Like Lassie on TV.

She went to the window and looked out. Under bright lights in the yard, the dogs circled and whined trying to pick up Dolly's scent from the rain-soaked ground.

Dolly wasn't found until dawn. The rain had stopped when they brought her home.

A little later, crouched by the window, Rita clapped her hands over her ears to shut out her mother's screams. She hadn't known that her self-possessed mother could make such sounds.

Later still her aunt Mary came upstairs, helped her get dressed and told her Dolly was dead.

Frozen in guilt, she couldn't cry or speak.

Her parents' door was shut.

"Dr. Lewis is with your mother," her aunt said on the way downstairs.

There was no one around now except for a policeman in the living room with her father and a neighbor woman in the kitchen getting Rita's breakfast.

But it was wasted effort. All she could manage to get down was a glass of milk and half a slice of toast.

Presently she was able to speak. "Where's Dolly now?" she asked.

"They took her away," Aunt Mary replied. "Dr. Lewis has to examine her body."

"When will I see Mama?"

"By-and-by. The doctor's giving her something to make her sleep."

"You poor child," the neighbor woman said.

It was the first word of sympathy Rita herself had been given. She broke down and sobbed hysterically.

Her father heard her and came out into the kitchen but did not gather her into his arms to offer comfort. He patted her on the head, said, "There, there, Rita," and returned to the living room.

He summoned her, though, as soon as her aunt had quieted her down.

"This is Lieutenant Hapenny," he said indicating the policeman. "He wants to ask you a few questions."

Questions from a policeman. In her terror Rita blurted out, "Hapenny? That's a funny kind of name."

"Rita!" her father said sharply.

The lieutenant only smiled. "Lots of people say that. It's the name I was born with, though, and there's not much I can do about it."

But his attempt to put her at ease did little good. Rigid in the doorway she said no, she didn't want to go in and sit down.

"That's okay," he said when her father would have insisted on it. "There's just a few things I want to ask you about, Rita. For instance, your daddy tells me you didn't see your little sister yesterday after you came in from playing outdoors with her. That right?"

"Yes." Rita stared at him saucer-eyed.

"Sir," her father reminded her.

"Yessir."

"And you didn't speak to her at all when she went upstairs—like asking what she was doing in your parents' bedroom?"

"I was reading."

"I see. The way it figures, she got your mother's dress out of the closet then. But what about the high-heeled shoe we found in the ravine? Must have been two of them—we haven't found the other one yet—where were they kept? Your father says it looks like one of the old shoes your mother let you play with."

"There's a box of dress-up shoes in Dolly's closet."

"Did you hear her in her room getting them?"

Rita shook her head.

"Must have been a pretty good book you had your nose buried in. . . . Let's go back to when you were outside together. Did your little sister say anything about dress-ups then?"

Little sister. "No—no sir." Little sister dead at the bottom of the ravine and Mama's dress all torn.

"So she just took it into her head when she got tired of playing outdoors by herself." The lieutenant shifted in his chair. "Funny thing for her to do without saying a word to you about it. Did the two of you ever play over by the ravine together?"

"A few times."

"All the more reason I'd expect her to ask you to go along. Shouldn't think it would be much fun, little tyke like her, going over there all by herself to play. Late in the day for it too."

"She didn't ask me," Rita said, mouth parched with fear.

"Funny thing for her to do," the lieutenant repeated not taking his eyes off Rita, trying, it seemed to her, to see inside her head, how much truthfulness there was in it.

But he couldn't really, truly see inside her head, all the lies she was telling. That was a crazy idea. It just came to her because she was so scared.

"Seems it's what she did, though," the lieutenant continued. "And got too near the edge of the ravine, stumbled maybe in those high-heeled shoes and fell. Too bad"—his eyes bored into Rita—"you weren't with her to run home and tell what happened so that we could have got her up out of there right away."

Rita burst into tears. "But I wasn't," she wailed. "I was here. I was upstairs in my room"—she wailed louder—"reading a book."

"Rita," her father began helplessly, but it was her aunt Mary who took charge rushing in from the kitchen. "Well now," she said drawing Rita close and looking reproachfully at the lieutenant. "Hasn't she told you all she can by this time?"

"Reckon so," he replied. "Sorry she got upset, ma'am."

But Rita wasn't sure the lieutenant believed her story. She was no more sure of it now than she was then. But it didn't matter all these years later sitting on her patio, doomed to be a captive of that awful time when Dolly died for the rest of her days.

It didn't seem fair, she thought wearily, getting up and going into the house. Hadn't she punished herself long enough for that great black sin committed more than twenty years ago? Not an adult sin, either, but one committed by an eight-year-old child terrified of being blamed for all of it.

No amount of rationalization, however, had lightened the load for her. But at least, she thought, going upstairs to bed, now that she had relived Dolly's death once again, it would recede into the past for a while. She was like the mediaeval monks who scourged themselves to get rid of their sins and then experienced an interlude of peace.

Even at that moment Dolly was fading out of her mind. She did not think of Winifred at all.

XXI

That Sunday night while Rita sat on her patio trapped in the past, Ted Parker called Janet from North Carolina.

"Well, sweetie," she said, "I hope you're calling to tell me you'll be coming back here soon."

"As a matter of fact, yes. This time for at least six to eight weeks."

"Good. We'll have to celebrate. When will you get here?"

"A week from today."

"Oh dear, not until then? I'm off all next weekend and it would be just great if we could get together."

"Well, it won't be Saturday night, that's for sure. I've got to go to a dinner meeting here before I leave."

"That means I won't see you the whole weekend!"

"Not necessarily. I should be able to break away from the meeting by ten o'clock and I plan to start out then. You know, have everything packed and in the car ahead of time and just take off. If I get in two or three hours' driving Saturday night I should be back in plenty of time for us to go out to dinner Sunday night. Hold it open for me. If there's any change in my plans I'll call you. Okay?"

"Wonderful. I'll stay close to the phone Sunday afternoon."

"That's the spirit," he said. "Oh, make us a reservation somewhere, will you?"

"My choice?"

"Right."

They talked a while longer. After they said good-by, Janet, stretched out on her bed where she had taken the call, propped the pillows under her head and thought about where they should go for dinner to celebrate Ted Parker's return.

Her choice, he had said. The Blue Grotto? Maybe. Not as interesting, though, as it would have been if Winifred worked there.

Had Rita asked her yet why she had lied about it? Would she ever ask her?

No way to find out. No use making up some excuse to call Rita. It would just lead to another snub from her.

There was, however, her aunt's birthday present. Now that it was June, she wouldn't be too much ahead of herself delivering it, would she? Once she was on the doorstep Rita would have to invite her in. As they sat and talked, she might be able to pick up some information about Winifred; perhaps find out if Rita had asked her yet where she really worked.

There was also the off-chance that Winifred herself would be home and Janet would at last get to meet her.

But somehow she didn't think this would happen, not after all the setbacks that had attended her efforts so far.

Winifred. Why had she lied about her job? That was the major question although there were many others, including her never being home when Janet called.

But puzzling over it did no good. She had done it often enough before and got nowhere. She would just have to wait and see what she could find out when she delivered Rita's present.

This coming Saturday she would go ahead with it. Call Rita first to make sure she was home and hang right up if she answered so as to arrive unannounced.

Go in the morning around ten o'clock. And what a bonus it would be if just this once, in spite of all her doubts that it would happen, Winifred was home too.

Maybe she would be. Maybe Saturday would be Janet's lucky day.

When Saturday came, lucky or not, it turned out to be a bright sunny day. The kind of day, Janet thought, getting up before nine, when Rita was bound to be home working in her garden.

Breakfast didn't take long. In her bare feet Janet padded around her small kitchen pouring juice, toasting an English muffin while water boiled for instant coffee.

No morning paper kept her at the table. She was fond of saying—dimple displayed in a pensive smile when she said it to men—that she didn't get the paper because there never seemed to be any good news in it. There was nothing she could do about all the awful things that happened in the world and they depressed her so much that she just didn't want to read about them.

By nine-thirty she was out of the shower starting to get dressed. Then she remembered that she hadn't called yet to check on whether or not Rita was home.

She dialed the number and let it ring and ring. When Rita answered at last, her voice sounded breathless as if from running.

Janet hung up the moment she said hello. Just as she had expected, Rita was working outdoors and had come rushing in to answer the phone.

What about Winifred? Well, if she was there, she might be sleeping late and not have heard it. There was no phone in her room, Janet recalled.

That was a funny thing too, now that she thought of it, one more of the many funny little things connected with Winifred. It seemed as if she would want a phone by her bed.

Maybe she'd got one since the time Janet was in her room. That was weeks ago, not very long after she had moved in. Maybe, if she wasn't home today, Janet could ask to use the bathroom as she had the other time and get a look in her room to see if she had a phone now on her nightstand.

Soon after ten o'clock Janet was ready to leave with Rita's birthday present tucked under her arm.

Starting her car, a new thought about Winifred's phone suddenly occurred to her. What if she'd had one of her own put in instead of just having an extension on Rita's line? If that was the case, if she had her own phone with her own separate number, it explained why Janet had never been able to reach her. With Rita at work, Winifred didn't answer her phone when it rang.

She should have thought of that long ago, Janet told herself, driving out of the parking lot and heading toward Route 7. When she got back from Rita's, she would call Woodbridge Information and ask if there was a phone listing for Winifred Lawton. Unless, in the meantime, she got a chance to look in Winifred's room.

When Janet called her Rita was in the garage getting out the lawn mower to cut the grass. It was annoying to hear the receiver click just as she said hello but it had happened often enough before. She really shouldn't bother rushing back into the house when she heard the phone ring; should be past the stage where she couldn't let it ring unanswered for fear that she might miss some special sort of call, something important.

She went back to the lawn mower and rolled it down the driveway to the front of the house. That was her regular routine cutting the grass. Mowing the front lawn first meant that if anything interrupted her before she got all of it cut, at least the grass out front would present a neat appearance from the street.

She yanked the cord to start the motor and resignedly set about her task, the one she disliked most in outdoor work.

By the time Janet arrived she had finished cutting the grass in front and on both sides of the house and was just starting to do the back. With the mower running, she didn't hear Janet's car turn in onto the driveway.

Janet braked to a stop a short distance in from the street. That was her habit whenever she visited Rita to make it more convenient to back out. No thought of inconveniencing anyone else who might arrive entered her mind.

She shut off the motor and listened to the sound of the lawn mower. The direction from which it came placed Rita at the far end of the back yard. The garage door was rolled up with Rita's car inside. There was no other car around. Winifred wasn't home.

Her glance went to the front door standing wide open. Was the screen door unlocked? And how long would it take Rita to work her way past the house to where she could see Janet's car in the driveway?

Janet had no idea, never having mowed a lawn in her life. But it seemed to her that if she could get inside she could allow herself a few minutes at least to run upstairs for a quick look around Winifred's room before making her arrival known to Rita.

And even if she got caught, she thought, easing her car door shut behind her and hurrying across the lawn to the front door, there was no way for Rita to make a big deal out of it. What could she say if Janet told her she was in such urgent need of the bathroom that she couldn't take time to announce her presence before rushing upstairs?

The screen door was unlocked, the handle turning under her hand. She went inside, the door closing itself behind her, and stood and listened for a moment to the lawn mower, not so loud a sound as it was outdoors.

For all her brashness, Janet felt a little nervous over the possibility of being caught in the middle of her spur-of-the-moment plan.

She raced upstairs, telling herself she would stay in Winifred's room just long enough to see if she'd had her own phone put in, take a look in the closet at the beautiful clothes Rita said she had and perhaps peek into her bureau drawers.

At the most, she would only stay three or four minutes. Then she would go back out the front door, collect Rita's present from her car and walk around the house to greet her as if she had just arrived.

The day was getting hot. Rita had no protection from the sun when she reached the middle of the back yard. Sweat ran down her forehead and stung her eyes. Stopping to wipe it off, she realized she was thirsty. She throttled down the mower and headed for the back door debating whether to settle for a glass of water or take a break for a beer. Just water for now, she decided, opening the screen door. The beer would taste much better when she had finished the lawn and could relax in the knowledge that it was done.

She stepped over the threshold and stopped short holding the door as she heard a sound—a footstep, wasn't it?—upstairs. She shut the door quietly and stood stock-still listening.

She heard the sound again. Yes, a footstep. Someone was up there.

But how—?

By the front door, of course. She had left it open, left the screen door unlocked when she went across the road before breakfast to get the paper.

She would never do that again. It didn't help right now, though, to think about being more careful in the future.

Rita glanced at the phone, her heart thudding. Would she be overheard if she called the police?

She might be. Better try first to find out more about who was upstairs moving around in Winifred's room. If she got caught listening at the foot of the stairs she could run outside.

Noiseless in her rubber-soled sneakers, she crossed the kitchen and living room to the front hall. Then through the door she saw Janet's car parked outside.

Fear gave way to red rage. Janet had sneaked into the house and gone upstairs to snoop around in Winifred's room!

How long ago? How much had she seen?

Everything, of course. It would take her no time at all to discover the truth about Winifred.

That searing thought sent Rita flying up the stairs.

Janet, opening bureau drawers, heard her too late to reach the doorway before Rita appeared in it crying, "You sneaky prying little bitch!"

Janet retreated a few steps toward the jog formed by the closet, built out from the wall. But as Rita advanced into the room Janet felt trapped there in the corner and edged around in front of the open closet door.

"What do you mean?" She tried to sound indignant. "I just got here a couple of minutes ago and I had to go to the bathroom so bad that I couldn't even stop to say hello."

"You call this the bathroom?" Rita's tone flayed her with contempt as her glance took in the bureau drawers pulled out, the closet door wide open. "You're not even a good liar, are you? Just a rotten little sneak."

"Is that so?" Janet went on the offensive her own temper flaring up. "Maybe I need some lessons in lying from you. You're the real expert at it. You really had me believing in your friend Winifred who'd come here to live with you. I swallowed the whole story, the beautiful divorcee who was a hostess at The Blue Grotto—my God, it drove me up the wall trying to figure out why she was never home, where she worked, why you'd never let me meet her—" Janet broke off laughing shrilly.

"Cut that out! There's nothing to laugh about."

"Isn't there? The touches you've added—like the pictures stuck in the mirror—would make anyone laugh. Who are those people anyway—the woman you said was Winifred, the wedding couple, the little girl?"

"They're none of your business," Rita cried furiously. "Nothing in this room is your business. The very idea of sticking your nose in here where you're not wanted. I could have you arrested for trespassing!"

"Go ahead and call the police," Janet mocked her. "Show them this room. Tell them about Winifred. Then you'll be the one they lock up."

"Don't you—don't you—dare say that," Rita stuttered choking with rage.

"Truth hurts, huh?" Janet felt that she had the upper hand now and turned away from Rita to look in the closet again. "Winifred's beautiful clothes!" Her laughter, shriller than before, rang through the room. She leaned against the door helplessly and gasped, "You're completely off your tree, Rita. Bughouse crazy, that's what you are."

"Shut up!"

But Janet was laughing too hard to notice the look on Rita's face that would have told her she had gone too far. "Comes of having no husband, doesn't it? Living alone, got to have somebody, pretend you have a roommate named Winifred—"

Rita snatched up the paper knife on the desk and lunged at her. "You miserable little bitch, I'll shut your mouth for good!"

Janet's laughter ended in a scream. She couldn't get past Rita to the door. She ran around to the far side of the bed trying to ward off the knife and screamed again at the top of her lungs.

It was the last sound she would ever make.

XXII

Rita came out of the room and closed the door. Moving slowly, cautiously, as if she might otherwise come apart, she went downstairs and out into the kitchen.

She drank two glasses of water, her throat so dry that one was not enough to quench the thirst that had brought her into the house a while ago. How long ago?

The clock said ten of eleven.

She washed her hands, dried them with meticulous care and sent an uncertain glance around the kitchen. Now what should she do?

She became aware of a steady drone from out in back. The lawn mower idling. She had not finished cutting the grass.

The first thing to do was to get that out of the way. Then she would think about what to do next.

She went outside and finished the rest of the lawn. Putting the mower back in the garage, it might have been any Saturday from spring until fall except that she omitted the hand clipping that usually completed her task. She took the clippers out of the basket, looked at the sharp blades with fastidious distaste and put them back.

"Maybe tomorrow," she said aloud as if her normal weekend routine would continue, as if the blood-red line that cut through it did not exist.

But there was finality in rolling down the garage door. Rita turned away from it and looked at Janet's car parked at the foot of the driveway.

She frowned over Janet's thoughtlessness in leaving it so near the road. If anyone else came there was hardly room to pull in behind it. She wasn't expecting anyone but still—

Were the keys in the ignition? She went down the driveway to look. Yes, they were there and a gift-wrapped package lay on the seat. Her present from Aunt Mary sent in a different world and time. Janet shouldn't have brought it. Rita had told her she would pick it up herself.

She got in behind the wheel, started the car and moved it up close to the garage door. Now there was plenty of room for anyone who might stop by.

She left the keys in the ignition when she got out and closed the car window in case it rained. No rain was predicted but it was just as well to be on the safe side.

Rita felt at loose ends after that, crossing the yard aimlessly. There must be something else she had to do. Her glance fell on the birdbath close to the back fence. It needed to be hosed out and filled with fresh water. And was there enough seed in the bird feeders?

Those small chores were taken care of all too soon. She wasn't wearing her watch. She went inside and looked at the clock. Only twenty minutes of twelve. The greater part of the day still lay ahead.

It turned out to be an endless one. She put on her watch to keep track of the time but that made it drag even more.

She felt thirsty again when she sat down on the shady side of the patio and brought out a can of beer. Sipping it slowly gave her something to do with herself.

At one o'clock the phone rang. It was Angie Hunt asking if she would be free for bridge that evening.

"No, I'm afraid not," Rita said.

She would never be free for anything again.

The day crept on. There was no shade on the patio as the sun climbed high overhead. Rita, staring into space, became conscious of how hot it was. She got another beer out of the refrigerator and carried one of the chairs across the yard to sit in the shade of a tree. It would be cooler in the house, she knew, but couldn't bring herself to go in.

The phone rang again. It was Mrs. Wheelock who said, "Rita, I just ran into a neighbor of mine whose sister is visiting her. I invited them over for a drink around five-thirty and I'd like to have you come too. Are you free?"

Free. That word again.

"No, I'm afraid not."

"Oh, that's too bad. . . ." Mrs. Wheelock hesitated, catching the lifeless note in Rita's voice, and then asked, "Is anything wrong?"

"Well, yes. Sort of a showdown with Winifred."

"Oh . . ." Mrs. Wheelock hesitated again but it didn't seem quite the moment to ask what had happened. She would hear all about it anyway Monday at the office, she thought, and let it go, saying, "I hope it works out all right."

"I don't see how it can," Rita said. "Enjoy your party anyway."

"We will. I'm sorry you won't be with us."

They said good-by and hung up.

The clock over the sink said quarter of two. She'd had nothing to eat since early breakfast but had no desire to eat now. She needed something, though, to take away the empty feeling inside her.

Another beer? That didn't have to be chewed and swallowed like food.

Three cans of beer were much more than she was used to. An hour later, the third can empty, she rested her head against the back of the chair and fell asleep.

It was past seven o'clock when she woke up. In the moment of waking it might have been any summer day at all, the sun far in the west, shadows long across the yard. But then the horror it had brought, Janet upstairs in Winifred's room, rushed in upon her. It couldn't be real; but it was.

Years ago when she was growing up her mother used to warn her about the fits of rage that sometimes overtook her. "Rita," she would say, "if you don't learn to control that temper of yours, one of these days you'll end up doing great harm to yourself or someone else."

Great harm. Would her mother use those same words if she knew what had happened to Janet that morning?

Of course. Wasn't killing the greatest harm of all that could be done to anyone?

She sprang to her feet. "Oh God, what am I going to do? Oh God—"

The next moment she burst into tears and sank down onto the chair again.

But when her fit of weeping was over the calm that had possessed her all that day returned. She carried her chair back to the patio and went indoors. She felt a little lightheaded from her long fast. She had to eat something. Soup and crackers at least.

Although it was only eight o'clock when she finished eating, she thought she might as well get ready for bed.

She kept her gaze averted from Winifred's room when she reached the top of the stairs. Daylight had faded from the upstairs hall, the setting sun that usually shone into it from Winifred's room cut off by the closed door.

Rita rushed through getting undressed and took a pillow and blanket off her bed. She would not sleep in it tonight. She would sleep downstairs on the sofa.

On her way down she remembered that she hadn't brought in the evening paper from the tube across the road but did not bother to go and get it. The last thing that concerned her tonight was what was happening in the rest of the world.

She made up a bed on the sofa and turned on the TV, not really to watch it but for company's sake.

Hour after hour she lay curled up in the blanket, not getting up to change the channel she had selected at random, letting the programs it offered roll over her unheeded.

Sometime after one o'clock her glazed eyes closed on the late movie and she fell asleep.

She was up at daybreak making breakfast, toast, coffee, a boiled egg, and forcing herself to eat it.

The house couldn't hold her afterward. She went outdoors into the sunrise, kicked off her slippers and walked around and around the yard, the grass heavy with dew, icy under her bare feet.

They were purple with the cold before she sat down on the patio, rubbing them to restore circulation and then putting her slippers back on.

She sat shivering in her thin robe but did not go back into the house. As the sun climbed higher it gradually warmed her flesh but had no effect on the coldness inside her.

Today wasn't like yesterday, though, when she had let time suspend itself. Today she had to have help, she knew, someone to tell her what to do about Janet.

The thought of it propelled her to her feet to walk around the yard again faster and faster, her pace quickening into a run, a frantic burst of speed that went on until she fell panting and distraught into a chair.

"Oh God, what shall I do?" she cried aloud, burying her head in her hands.

The cry brought no answer. Rita raised her head and looked wildly in all directions. The peaceful setting, a robin splashing extravagantly in the birdbath, a cardinal chip-chipping from a fence post, children's voices coming from a distance made what had happened yesterday seem all the more unreal, another of the nightmares that had afflicted her in the recent past.

Go upstairs, she told herself, open that door, make sure it isn't one of them.

She started toward the house, saw Janet's car in the driveway, and dropped down in hopeless despair on the back steps. It was not a nightmare that she was going through. Janet's car was there because her body lay upstairs in Winifred's room.

Rita stayed where she was, half-sitting, half-lying on the back steps, lacking the will to move, losing track of time and presently, her sense of reality. . . .

Janet's car didn't have to mean that she was dead upstairs. Winifred could have borrowed it yesterday because she'd had trouble with her own car. No reason, therefore, that it shouldn't be standing in the driveway. After all, this was where she lived, wasn't it? If there'd been a double garage, she would have put the car inside next to Rita's.

Maybe not, though. She wasn't always too well organized. Look at the time she had torn her room apart and that other time when she had got hold of a knife and Rita had cut herself taking it away from her.

But no, that wasn't exactly the way those things had occurred. . . .

Crouched on the back steps, Rita tried to get them straight in her mind. Winifred wasn't to blame for them because she didn't exist.

But of course she did. Hadn't she been living here since March working at The Blue Grotto?

No, they had told Janet she didn't work there.

Where did she work then?

It didn't matter because she would never work anywhere again. She lay dead upstairs in her room.

But how could that be—the body of someone who didn't exist?

The phone rang. Rita paid no attention to it at first but it rang and rang until at last she answered it.

It was Mrs. Wheelock concerned over her after their talk yesterday.

At the sound of her voice Rita broke down, reaching out to her as a drowning person would reach for a life raft. She was so competent she would know what to do, would take care of it all.

"Oh, Mrs. Wheelock," she said tears pouring down her face, "something terrible's happened. It's just too much for me. Can you come right away?"

"Yes, of course." Mrs. Wheelock wasted no time on questions. "Just hold everything," she said. "I'll get there fast as I can."

"Thank you." Rita hung up and sagged against the counter. Not for long, though. She couldn't bear being in the house and went back outdoors.

The first thing Mrs. Wheelock saw when she turned in at the driveway was Janet's car. Her eyebrows went up. Janet here? She had assumed that whatever was wrong was connected with Winifred.

She pulled up behind the car and saw Rita huddled in a chair on the patio. She stood up slowly as Mrs. Wheelock hurried toward her, taking in the way she looked, still in robe and nightgown, hair disheveled, dazed expression on her tear-blotched face.

"Why Rita," she said gently. "What's happened. What's the matter?"

Rita looked at her narrowing her eyes as if to identify someone at a distance.

"It's Winifred," she said unsteadily. "She's dead. Upstairs in her room."

"What?"

"She's dead. I killed her."

"Oh no." The competence Rita was relying on deserted Mrs. Wheelock for the moment. She sank onto the nearest chair. "You—killed her?"

"Yes. With the paper knife on her desk. It's very heavy and sharp, you know. It's old. It belonged to Aunt Edna."

"Dear God," Mrs. Wheelock said under her breath and aloud, keeping her voice firm, "Are you sure she's dead? Perhaps she's just hurt. Perhaps if we got a doctor right away—?"

Rita shook her head, the dazed look fixed on her face. "It wouldn't do any good. She's been there since yesterday. She's—in the closet, I think."

Mrs. Wheelock took a deep breath and got to her feet. "Shall I go up and see?"

"Yes. I haven't gone near her myself. I just shut the door."

On her way into the house Mrs. Wheelock's glance fell on Janet's car, momentarily forgotten in the shock of what she had been told. Where was Janet? She started to ask but then let it go. Poor overwrought Rita had answered enough questions for the moment. Janet could wait until she had seen for herself what the situation was upstairs.

Rita tagged along behind her not wanting to go into the house but even more reluctant to let Mrs. Wheelock out of her sight.

She hung back pressed against the wall when they got upstairs.

Mrs. Wheelock opened the door. Janet's body, on the far side of the bed, wasn't visible from the doorway. The first thing Mrs. Wheelock saw was the bureau drawers pulled out. A few tentative steps forward revealed that they were empty.

There was an odd unpleasant smell in the room even though the windows were partly open. It chilled her as she identified it. It was the smell of death.

The closet door to her right was wide open pushed all the way back to the wall behind it. That was where she would find Winifred Lawton's body.

Mrs. Wheelock moved toward it reluctantly bracing herself for what she would see.

The next moment she was in a state of total bewilderment looking into the closet. There was no body in it. There was nothing at all except a child's blue plaid dress.

She tried to collect her thoughts. Did Winifred have a child the dress belonged to? But where were her own clothes? Packed to move out? And where was Winifred herself—or rather, her body?

It had to be either under the bed or on the other side of it. Anywhere else in the room it would be in plain sight.

As Mrs. Wheelock turned away from the closet her numbed gaze fell again on the empty bureau drawers. Winifred's intention to leave must have brought on the scene that led to her death.

With the hall door open, the smell of it was not as strong now in the room.

Mrs. Wheelock braced herself for the second time, walked around the bed and saw the body—Janet's body, not Winifred's—curled up in foetal position on the floor.

"Oh God—!" Her hand reached out to the bedpost for support.

Janet lay in a pool of dried blood, hands and neck gashed, the handle of the paper knife protruding from her back.

Trying to pull herself together, Mrs. Wheelock concentrated on the paper knife. Aunt Edna's, Rita had said. Not Winifred's.

There was nothing of hers in the room, no clothes in the closet, nothing in the bureau drawers. . . .

Mrs. Wheelock's whirling thoughts steadied. Winifred hadn't packed to leave. There was no such person. There never had been. Rita had made her up.

"Rita," she called out. And again, in a fading voice, "Rita—"

"Yes?" Rita came as far as the door and eyed her emptily.

"Why?" Mrs. Wheelock asked turning to look at her. "What did Janet do that you killed her?"

"She sneaked up here to snoop. I caught her in the middle of it." A faint trace of the outrage she had felt yesterday echoed in Rita's voice.

"You killed her over that?"

"She said awful things. She laughed and laughed at me. She said I was crazy fixing this room up to make people think it was Winifred's. She said it was because I had no husband. She said they'd lock me up. I couldn't stand the way she kept laughing at me, looking in the closet at Dolly's dress."

"Dolly—?" Mrs. Wheelock, in the stress of the moment, couldn't place the name.

"My little sister who died. Not from her fall, the doctor said, but from shock and exposure. She could have been saved, he said, if she had been found right away."

"Oh yes, Dolly . . ."

"That's what we always called her. Daddy started it when she was a baby. She looked like a little doll, he said. But her real name was Winifred."